A Love to Die For

Part 1

Leigh Oakley

"Sometimes our worst enemy lies within our own mind."

Chapter 1

The digits of the alarm clock jolted from 5.57 to 5.58. Sophie had been watching this countdown for almost an hour whilst swallowing silent sobs, in this all too familiar start to another dark January morning. One more blink forced the inevitable overflow and tears trickled over the bridge of her nose into her other eye and down onto the damp pillow.

Yesterday had been another nail in the coffin for her and Carl. Something she was finding more and more difficult to deny. Sunday afternoon, mid hike, on the top of a mountain he had taken her hand in his in a symbolic way as he absorbed the view before them.

He was sharing the moment with the woman he loved, and her hand had remained dutifully but loosely in his, as she returned his smile. Anger and jealousy gripped her chest, for he was clearly feeling something she would sell her soul to feel. To feel exactly what he was feeling in that moment, to experience the love and adoration she saw in his eyes. She imagined how perfect it would be for two people to be that much in love simultaneously.

The surge of disappointment rose from her stomach like a pan of boiling milk, spilling ruthlessly into her thoughts, dissolving the beauty of the view and exposing her empty heart. The awful truth she had been fighting for so long had risen once more and the power of it was undeniable, this yearning for something else. Something more.

A whisper from the soulmate she had yet to meet, the love who is still out there somewhere but whom she might never find. Her hand dropped sub-consciously from Carl's. Immediately he frowned as she quickly pretended to adjust her shoe with the offending hand and returned it quickly to his. Once reunited she kissed it playfully as she pushed the doubt back down inside her as best she could, the way she always had.

It was this yearning that occupied Sophie's mind as she hit the snooze button for the third time in a vain attempt to delay the start of another empty day.

She had been doing this now for weeks, probably months. Trying to dispel the sinking feeling in her stomach followed by the tightness and fluttering in her chest telling her that all was not well. But what it was that wasn't well she wasn't exactly sure. The wedding plans? The wedding itself? Marriage in general? Her and Carl? Love? (whatever that was) Life? She pulled the duvet over her head and pondered that the problem could be her. Depression maybe?

In these days of uncertainty and emotional turmoil she had no idea how small her troubles were. It seemed unimaginable that one day, a day not too far away, she would look back on these days with envy and longing because in comparison to what was to come, these were her happy days.

"You late?" Carl droned sleepily throwing an arm in her direction, his hand landing carelessly on her breast.

"Not especially." She gritted her teeth as he gave her nipple a playful squeeze and smacked his lips.

Her heart sank further. What should have felt like an amusing playful gesture, felt annoying and degrading and the blame was impossible to apportion. Quickly she averted the issue by sliding from under his half-hearted advance.

"Want a cuppa?"

"Is the pope a catholic?" As he said the words, she lip-synced his response sarcastically as she wrapped her robe around her and headed for the kitchen. He was so predictable, so bland, so boring.

As she waited for the kettle to boil, she opened the 'odds and ends' drawer and searched for the notepad she took out far too regularly. The first page was divided into two columns FOR and AGAINST. For and against what exactly, she didn't know, but she had made the lists and discarded them so many times the imprints could usually be used as a prompt for the new page. This was something her mother had encouraged her to do when making important or difficult decisions. It had worked brilliantly for choosing a college, a holiday destination or a car but she wasn't sure it was exactly right for selecting a husband.

Under the '*for*' column she wrote... 'Easy going, caring, works hard, good father material, listens to me, doesn't gamble or womanise, gets on with my family, fun in company, loves animals, likes to party, never grumpy, always remembers valentine's day.'

She stopped for a moment to make the tea, quickly returning, once again to the exercise that would prove, beyond all reasonable doubt that she was just being stupid and finnicky. The '*against*' column was as short as it always was and contained nothing of any substance.... 'Forgets to take the rubbish out, leaves food cartons in his car, hardly ever gets up first.'

It was a pitiful list of meagre crimes but what if the against list didn't need to contain an abundance of serious offences to tip the scale? What if one single 'against' item outweighs everything else and what if that one single item was this feeling she dreads every morning. Picking up the pen she added an entry on the column in giant letters 'THAT FEELING'

Pushing the pad back in the drawer she set about getting ready for work and wondered if she should talk about this to her friends. Even a hint of doubt might set tongues wagging and they would become consumed by her predicament. They would be having those late-night conversations with their partners about how the wedding may be off. One thing she had learned about human nature was its appetite for revelling in the misfortune of others. She loved her friends dearly and she knew they wished her no harm, but she had often found herself gossiping to Carl excitedly about a friend's problem. After all, its human nature to want to feel more fortunate than the next person and that kind of smugness and contentment is derived from comparison with others, especially those with problems. She had no wish to be the provider of that kind of therapy right now.

She had always acted blissfully happy in public from the moment Carl proposed and unless she was absolutely sure there was a problem, she was not going to reveal any cracks in her persona of ecstatic bride-to-be. Her mother's words resounded "Never tell anyone your troubles – twenty percent don't care and the other eighty are glad you have them"

At least it was Friday – dress down Friday meaning she could pull on her jeans and a sweater, tug her dark wavy hair into a casual ponytail and not worry about running over the icy car park in high heels. Holding her toast between her teeth she retrieved her list from the drawer and added to the 'FOR' column "Never complains about what I wear or asks me to dress sexily. "She spoke the words as slowly as she wrote them then shook her head in dismay at what she had resorted to.

"Tea baby." She whispered, delivering the ritualistic morning kiss which had long since lost any real meaning in the drudgery of routine.

"Thanks darling." His response, on the other hand, though equally predictable was not lacking in feeling or sincerity.

She paused at the door, caught in a moment of guilt, considering if some display of affection was advisable, something to even up the warmth of the exchange but she couldn't bring herself to add anything, and slipped off to work with a casual remark

"Don't forget I am having a drink with the girls after work."

"Okey Dokey – have fun lover."

Her stomach turned another somersault as she started the engine and headed into work.

The day went quickly as most Friday's did in a hotel. It was hardly the height of season but there were always the weekenders taking advantage of bargain winter rates for a short break on the east coast. She had been in the position of trainee manager now for three years and was hoping for a promotion to assistant manager later in the year. Unless they filled the position externally there was only one other rival for the role. Tim, dim Tim, as she called him under her breath, but not because he lacked intelligence, in fact he was considerably her superior academically but, as with most spotty graduates, he had zero personality, people skills or sense of humour.

Closing down her computer at exactly six pm she hurried through the lobby and out into the cold dark evening, zipping her padded jacket right up to her chin. The light of one of the few restaurants staying open out of season guided her along the sea front. As she strode purposefully, battling the bitter wind, heavy with sea fret, she could just make out the familiar faces of her friends already engrossed in cheerful conversation. She paused for a moment - Niki, a junior Manager at a holiday park was chatting whilst toying with one of the small black ringlets she left uncaptured from her tightly coiled bun, whilst Kelly sucked a cocktail through a straw, clearly pre-occupied with a group of men over Niki's left shoulder. She was however, nodding enthusiastically, eyes wide as saucers if only to emphasize her newly purchased false lashes. Kelly was the epitome of her profession, a beautician in every stereo typical sense of the label. Bottle blonde, impeccable make up, false nails, lashes, breasts. Heart of gold but head mostly in the clouds or obsessing over her appearance.

Sophie paused for a moment and smiled. Nothing felt more like home than this sight before her. She knew that these years, the ones after college but before husbands and children are those most reminisced, usually with the soulful regret that they were neither recognised nor fully appreciated at the time. For this reason, she took a moment to do just that, to soak up the moment on this dark cold sea front, looking into the warmth of a lively pub with her best friends waiting as they did every Friday night. She wanted to commit it to memory, to print it on her heart in glorious technicolour before breaking the spell. As she moved forward her stomach churned again. There it was again. The sickening feeling that times were about to change. Probably due to her conceited belief that she deserved more. Probably not for the better.

Chapter 2

Running up the few steps and throwing open the door into the warmth, she shouted excitedly, and both girls squealed back, the way they always did as she pushed her way through the crowd to buy the round of drinks she knew by heart. Placing them on the high table they had occupied by the window she pulled up a bar stool and tried to catch up on the conversation.

She rubbed her hands and blew into them as the warmth of the room returned feeling to her nose and ears. These nights with the girls were what she looked forward to all week and surely that can't be right? She thought she had been listening, paying attention, until a prolonged silence caused her to take a look around.

"You ok Sophie"? Niki cocked her head to emphasise her concern.

"Sure, why?"

"Why?! "shrilled Kelly, "because we have been watching you for ten minutes without talking and you didn't even notice"

Her shallow giggle was in stark contrast to Niki's frown.

"What's up Sophie?"

"Nothing – just a busy day."

Niki raised her eyebrows disbelievingly.

"Ok. Just not been sleeping so well."

"Why not?" Kelly asked distractedly. She wasn't interested in a reply as she smiled at the man on the next table.

"Can I ask you something?" Sophie drew in breath and gave a big sigh "How do you know if you are in love?" and there it was. The big secret she had decided to keep to herself fell from her lips with less consideration than a comment on the weather.

It was a simple question, a common question, yet on this day from this person it exploded like a grenade. Silence followed. For several seconds the question hung over the table as the impact was assessed, and the enormity digested.

Kelly was the first to speak. Ill-considered words carelessly delivered. She offered them unashamedly and innocently and consequently the truth and honesty of them was undeniable.

"My mum used to say, if you have to ask if you love someone then the answer is probably 'no'."

Niki shot her a reprimanding glare and Kelly shrugged in defence.

"I know that I love him," Sophie was quick to confirm "but what about being in love?"

Niki sighed as she looked again in Kelly's direction. Kelly had averted her eyes which were filled with tears.

"I think the same principle probably applies." Niki said gently as she put her hand on Sophie's noticing that it was shaking, "How long have you been feeling like this?"

"Not sure. A few weeks, a couple of months, maybe longer, forever? Oh, I don't know I just know that the wedding is all arranged now but I just don't feel the least bit excited about it."

"That doesn't mean you don't want to be married to Carl though does it? Maybe you just don't rate all the fuss"?

"No Nik. I love the fuss. It's all I ever dreamed of. Big dress, big church, flowers, photos. The kiss and the first dance. It's just so romantic. It takes my breath away just to think of sharing that moment with someone."

"But not with Carl?"

"Not with Carl." She bit her lip to stop it quivering.

Niki pushed her wine towards her friend and gave her hand a squeeze. "Don't worry. Everything will be fine. Drink up and we'll try to help you get back into the swing of it. Maybe you should write a list of pros and cons?"

Sophie laughed out loud and pulled various almost identical lists from her handbag and threw them at Niki.

The two girls grinned and hugged spontaneously while Kelly frowned resentfully in the mirror at a strand of hair which was in urgent need of recapture.

"So, what box does Carl fail to tick?" Niki was trying to lighten the mood, but Pandora's box had been opened and its contents could not be so easily re-contained.

"That's just it. All boxes are ticked. On paper this should be the realisation of my fucking dream."

"But..?" Niki was a little taken aback, Sophie never swore.

"But it's just not how I imagined it to be. ".

No one spoke as Sophie drew another deep breath and gulped a mouthful of wine

"Ok, ever since I was old enough to understand the concept of Princes and Princesses and bloody 'Happy Ever Afters', broken hearts and a love worth dying for I just expected that love would be this great big.." her hands flew apart dramatically, "hurricane of emotion. That it would grasp my heart with such force it would feel physical. I want a love that I would die for. One love. A love I can't live without."

"And that's not how you feel?" Niki's tone reflected the obvious.

"I'm a million miles from it. I mean I would feel sad to lose Carl, I think. I'd probably feel jealous if he found another love, but I'd certainly not get into bed and die of a broken heart."

Kelly looked horrified "You want something that would make you feel so wretched?"

"Yes.Yes I do"

"Well," Kelly frowned, "anything that could make you want to die is far too dangerous I think."

Sophie smiled at Kelly's inability to conceive true love but at the same time marvelled at the type of wisdom that would surely be applauded by every heartbroken lover who has ever walked the planet.

"So why did you agree to marry him?" Kelly's tone was almost reprimanding

There was a knowing, and somewhat uncomfortable glance between Sophie and Niki

"What?"

Niki and Sophie looked at each other once more but then Niki reluctantly revealed the ridiculous truth.

"It was a clairvoyant. "

"What?"

Niki continued "Sophie went to see a clairvoyant last year and she said that she'd have a son with her current boyfriend."

Kelly stared at Sophie in disbelief "Were you having doubts even back then? I mean why would you want someone to tell you what you are going to do?"

Sophie tried to explain but Kelly's question had hit a nerve. "I asked if I would stay with my boyfriend and she said we would have a son together, so I thought that was meant to be. I mean she had a really good track record of getting it right."

"Well maybe that's because people like you do what she says," Kelly laughed "surely you don't believe all that mumbo jumbo?"

Sophie suddenly felt quite stupid "I didn't believe at first, but she knew all sorts of things she could never have known, personal things, and by the time I left I totally believed her."

Kelly was still shaking her head in disbelief when Niki decided to intervene.

"Never mind how you got here. What will you do now?" Niki's question was little more than a whisper

"I have no idea. Once I've started that ball rolling there'll be no going back. It's not like I can say I need more time. It's wedding on or wedding off. Then what if I regret it and so much damage has been done? He'll never love me the same again, so completely, will he? What if my great love never comes along? What if this feeling I am waiting for is no more than a myth?"

"It isn't." The voice was male and came from a few feet away

The three friends all turned in the direction of a group of men one of whom was making unnerving eye contact with Sophie.

"Sorry?" She retorted

"It isn't a myth."

"Just like that isn't a chat up line?" she laughed

But the pain was so visible on his face that Sophie felt instant and deep regret at her accusation and realised it had sounded somewhat conceited.

"I'm sorry."

"It's ok," he smiled weakly, "I just thought you should know that the kind of love you were talking about does exist but fortunately it only attacks a very very small percentage of us. Believe me, to have it and lose it is heaven and hell."

"You're saying I should settle for less than heaven?"

"Absolutely."

"How long did it take you to recover?"

He laughed sarcastically, "I hope to recover one day but my recovery is now five years in."

"And there has been no one else?

"On the contrary there has been everyone else! I have tried to replace her, reinvent her, to recreate her in every woman I have met and drove every one of them away. Years ago, they would say I was bewitched!! There's just nothing that compares to it, no other woman can do anything right. Either they don't say the right thing (the thing she would say) they don't laugh at the right time (the time she would laugh) they don't play (the way only she could) they don't measure up because she was the perfect fit for me. It's like everyone else is cast in the wrong role and don't know their lines or something. Don't think there will ever be a new leading lady for me, but I keep hoping and holding the relentless auditions."

All three women were also bewitched – by the visible intensity of his torment. This poor extremely good-looking man was truly a tortured soul.

"More drinks I think." Niki interjected, desperate to change the subject and the mood.

"You know the worst thing of all?" He sighed, not waiting for a response "she treated me like shit in the end. She was very clear about her feelings, but it didn't damn well change mine. The cruellest and most ironic thing of all is that when you genuinely love someone it doesn't matter what they do to you. It seems the more they hate you the more desperate you are to win their love back, their affection, their bloody approval. It's sick. It's what stalkers are made of!"

His captive audience were wide-eyed and a little unsettled until he broke into a smile.

"Don't worry. It's under control now but I wanted to warn you to be careful what you wish for."

Instantly one of his friends started to pull him away "Please excuse him. Whisky always conjures up the love monster. Then again, so does everything else."

He gently guided the man away who looked back at Sophie as he was jostled towards the bar

"I'm sorry luv. Didn't mean to spoil your night."

"Well thank you for the advice," Sophie smiled, suddenly feeling a little better "who's round is it?"

"Well, you've cheered up." Niki sounded pleasantly surprised.

"Well let's hope it's because she's taken heed of that awful story and has decided to stick with Carl. Lovely reliable Carl." even the way Kelly was describing him made Sophie's heart sink again.

"So, what if a voodoo woman did tell you to marry him, I think she probably had a point." Kelly smiled then quickly applied a bit more lip gloss and headed for the bar, "my round!"

As the evening went on, spirits were lifted by alcohol and funny stories from work but as the Friday after work drinkers began to leave for home or night clubs Sophie watched the man head off with his group of friends out into the night and couldn't help but notice so much about him. Things she would probably never have seen before.

As his three friends play punched and head-locked each other along the pavement he walked alongside politely unengaged in their high spirits. There was no spring in his stride, his head was down, and his hands hung limply by his side. Occasionally he made half-hearted attempts to join in with a high five or a gentle shove but so lacking in energy she concluded these were forced acts with the sole aim of preventing the dreaded suggestions to 'cheer up' or 'get a life' or some other futile cliché wielded by the unknowing, the unenlightened or the blissfully ignorant.

This was one of many fun boys' nights out he could only ever aspire to being a part of until his recovery commenced, if ever it would.

Sophie had no idea why she suddenly felt more positive. Was it because she had been convinced to play it safe and avoid being like this man or was it because he had confirmed that the type of love she longed for was out there?

She knew very well of the consequences that often come from ignoring sound advice and she had received it in bucketloads over the last few hours. Advice that should have placed her firmly back on her comfortable path yet there was something far more compelling in play. The little voice that had whispered to her in the night, just loud enough to plant some doubt was now screaming at her to follow her heart. To hell with comfortable reliable marriage, she wanted more, she needed more, and she deserved more.

Yes, ignoring sound advice could have serious consequences but as she put on her coat and headed out into the night air, she could never have conceived just how severe those consequences would turn out to be, nor the magnitude of the devastation that would follow.

Chapter 3

The weekend was as uneventful as any other. Shopping, housework, polite conversation, avoidance of wedding talk where possible, routine love making and time on her own on Sunday morning while Carl went to play football.

A welcome distraction for Sophie was putting together a presentation for Monday. This was her opportunity to impress some senior executives from head office and she was quite excited about tabling here ideas to improve customer service for the forthcoming season. Not only was it a chance at promotion but it temporarily shoved a spoke in the wheels of spinning thoughts inside her head and, if nothing else, it prevented her from writing any more lists!

She worked most of the day on it, taking full advantage of the excuse to ignore Carl when he returned cold and muddy. In fact, she had exploited the situation to the extent that by supper time she was quite excited about presenting her masterpiece. Having just celebrated the millennium she felt sure 2000 was going to be a momentous year for her as she neatly folded her notes and saved her slides to a floppy disc, so she could print them at work in the morning. She felt quite smug. She hadn't felt like this since the odd occasions at school when she put extra effort into her homework.

After only a brief interlude in which she stopped, to slop out a stew unceremoniously onto plates around 7 pm, she had worked constantly. Carl eventually took the hint, huffed and went to bed. She smiled. She knew this would give her the opportunity to sneak in later and turn her back to him without having to engage in any gestures of affection. She was right. He was snoring loudly by the time she slid gently under the duvet beside him.

Monday morning started the same as any other but today the sinking feeling wasn't as bad, as it was negated by the butterflies in her stomach. Partly caused by the ordeal ahead but mainly by the new dream of a soaring career she was inadvertently nurturing in her sub-conscious. Her ritual of tea making to shower to car was identical to every other workday, but her resentment of Carl was substantially lessened by her enthusiasm and anticipation for her presentation. Her sub-conscious was momentarily thwarted as she considered marriage to Carl once again. Perhaps she had just been lacking something to focus on. Perhaps there was nothing wrong with her relationship. She smiled in acceptance of the theory. Carefully pulled on her hold-up stockings, keeping her nails well-away from the delicate fabric. Today her appearance must be perfect from her silk blouse, pencil skirt with matching tailored jacket to her polished high heels and classic hair bun. She set off for work confident in the knowledge that she had some excellent self- funding ideas and couldn't wait to share them.

She set up the meeting room early, printed off her acetates, checked the computer was behaving and was on speaking terms with the projector (which it often wasn't), and ran through her slides to make sure none had escaped from her disc. She then sat down with a cup of coffee in nervous anticipation.

Her Manager, Paul was the first to arrive followed by two executives from head office and finally her colleague Tim who had obviously been invited without her knowledge.

The meeting room was very grand, freshly polished and adorned with refreshments fit for the executive status of her audience. A large fruit platter took centre stage on the boardroom table surrounded by company logo notepads and pens which had been set out with precision on leather writing mats.

She took her place at the head of the table next to the projector and instead of the unworthy nervous persona she was expecting to overwhelm her she felt suddenly important, worthy and empowered. She cleared her throat and introduced herself. She had intended to appeal to their sense of compassion by being humble. Carl had advised her to get them on side by acting insecure and nervous but his experience as a car mechanic hardly qualified him to give advice on delivering a presentation and she was going to do no such thing. This was her moment; she knew her stuff and she was going to own it.

Her voice was steady, audible and unhurried as she confidently delivered her outline noticing the shock on Tim's face from which her confidence grew as she moved from slide to slide. Questions and comments came in abundance and each one was carefully and calmly addressed. She had taken her moment and she knew it.

As the meeting finished and she was collecting her notes, her line Manager gave her a knowing wink. She knew she had been sickeningly flying the company flag. Relentlessly blowing smoke up the arses of everyone in the room but she didn't care. Today she was the corporate 'goody two shoes' but it's how people rise to the top and she was not going to apologise for it.

Tim rolled his eyes in repulsion of her 'teacher's pet' smugness and for a moment she felt a tiny bit embarrassed at wearing her halo so blatantly, but she was not going to allow envy to tarnish her moment of success. Not today.

Later that day she was asked back to Paul's office who passed on the praise from the executive team who had committed to considering some of her ideas and they had also endorsed a small pay rise in recognition of her entrepreneurial spirit. She thanked him and hid the ear to ear grin as she left his office.

She couldn't wait to call Carl. To give him the news and ask to meet him after work for a drink to celebrate. She mused that this was a positive sign in their relationship – surely wanting to celebrate her success with Carl established him as her partner. The first person she thought about when she had something good to share.

"That's great baby. Yes, I'll meet you in usual bar at six thirty."

He seemed warm and excited for her, and she felt even more positive, deciding that any doubts were most definitely misplaced and based on some childhood fantasy a world away from the reality of real life and real people.

She made a quick visit to the toilets before leaving work for her date with Carl, making sure that her makeup was ok and for a quick brush up in general. She smiled at this next positive sign of wanting to look her best. Arriving at six fifteen she got the drinks in and sat at the bar to wait for his familiar face to appear in the crowd.

"Oh God how fickle am I?" she muttered to herself an hour later when Carl was now back on her 'at risk' list after standing her up for a breakdown by text long after he was already late!

As she frantically typed the extent of her annoyance into her phone, the contents of her handbag spilled onto the floor, but she was too intent on finishing her message to be interrupted. Her face must have been contorted in anger as a cheerful voice sounded from the stool on her right

"Oh dear, that doesn't look good."

She raised her eyes to meet a smiling face offering her retrieved belongings in his open hands. The man looked familiar, yet she really couldn't place him. He probably just reminded her of someone, yet the feeling was one of bumping into an old friend.

"Do I know you?"

"Not yet." He winked cheekily.

His behaviour was arrogant and pushy but from someone who looked like an old friend she found it refreshingly amusing.

She was about to explain that her boyfriend had let her down but for some reason she edited the planned sentence and omitted the word boy.

It wasn't as if this man was particularly good looking – he was very over-weight, hair not very well styled, clothes smart but average yet there was just a strong aura of importance about him.

"Is it finders' keepers then?" He smiled, still holding the entire contents of her bag.

She glanced down and was horrified to see that the poor guy was holding a tampon among his spoils.

"Sorry – err thanks." She scooped everything back into her open bag desperately hoping he hadn't noticed, though she could tell from his eyes that he had. Eyes which were engaged with hers to the extent that she felt unsettled, disturbed almost, and still could not stop wondering if she knew him from somewhere.

"Since your friend isn't here shall we have another drink?" He cocked his head on one side in a sort of innocent plea.

Normally she would never accept a drink from a stranger, but she accepted without hesitation and nipped off to the toilets while he took care of it. Was her willingness the result of her need to punish Carl? Punish him for standing her up, for missing her celebration or perhaps it was her anger towards him for resurrecting the uncertainty she thought she had put to bed.

"What the hell are you doing?" She muttered to her reflection as she started to titivate her appearance. Her self-reprisal did not prevent the lipstick from gliding over her lips, the eye liner from tracing the outline of her eyelids nor the comb from tidying her hair.

Her reflection had no time to answer for she was already speeding back to her new acquaintance through the mist of hastily sprayed perfume. The expensive one Carl had bought her for Christmas. As she sped back into the crowd, her heart sank for a moment when she failed to spot him, assuming he had simply left, but as a young man leant forward, she caught a glimpse of the bright orange tee shirt that she had found so startlingly humorous. She sighed. All was well.

They chatted for a few minutes about his job as project manager at an International Bank, a subject which would ordinarily bore her into a coma, but she was hanging on his every word like a besotted student of a crush worthy professor, carefully watching his mouth as he spoke. How easy it is to absorb and understand even the dullest of information when you are hell bent on making an amazing impression. She heard herself asking questions about things she thought she had no ability to comprehend, but the need to engage with this man harnessed every morsel of her concentration. He, on the contrary spoke to her as casually as passing time with an old friend and just as his smile warmed her, his eyes intrigued her, and his cheeky winks amused her. This was, by far, the most magnetic person she had ever met and with each exchange he was rising dangerously on the pedestal before her at an alarming rate. Her head had zero success in reasoning with her heart.

"Why are you behaving like a groupie?" This time the silent question was not to her reflection but to this unknown flirtatious being who had taken over her body.

There was no reply from this inner being for it was on some rampage of its own, unstoppable and hell bent on fuelling the momentum of this soaring rocket. The exchanges were becoming more personal, witty, ambiguous, and compelling – who said the art of conversation was dead?

Suddenly the bar bell rang, and she realised it was closing time. She couldn't believe they had lost several hours engrossed in this addictive conversation but nor did she want it to end just yet. They were only just getting started.

She checked her phone and noticed eight missed calls from Carl.

"Damn it!" She knew she needed to go home, and she also knew she would need a better reason than to admit she had been talking to a man all evening.

As they left the building, he held out her coat and she spun into it back round to face him. There was a second, it can't have been longer than a second when she looked up into his face and a hundred questions needed no answer. She knew that no matter what tomorrow would bring, no matter what the consequence, she would seize this moment, this moment that may never come again and which may never ever feel this perfect.

Without speaking she held his eye contact for this one second and she was sure she could hear his heart pounding as loudly as hers. He took her hand in his and kissed it gently as he led her out into the cold night air. He walked proudly, confidently, almost arrogantly and she felt her body shudder with the thrill of it.

The car park was almost empty and as she loosened her grip on his hand and started heading towards her forlorn lonely little car nestled under some overhanging trees in the far corner, he tightened his and slowed her. She acted surprised but had been hoping he would do exactly that.

As she turned towards him with a pretence of puzzlement on her face, he leaned against a large sports car the make of which she was totally oblivious of but hoped from the way he was abusing it that it did belong to him.

"Would you like to sit in and finish talking for a few minutes?"

"Do you need to ask?" She was thinking but luckily her response was interrupted by what was left of her self- respect. "Well, it is very cold and if it's just for a few minutes!"

He smiled in acknowledgement of the game they were playing and opened the passenger door for her. The wind was gusting fine rain against her legs and she was grateful of the warmth and comfort of his immaculate car, feeling relieved he hadn't asked to sit in her dumpster on wheels. He jumped in quickly beside her and shuddered as he rubbed his hands together for warmth before taking hers once more. Through the windows they could just make out the silhouettes of the bar staff hurrying out of the staff entrance, shouting their hurried goodbyes as they scattered in different directions like fleeing cats.

In the darkness they sat and talked a little more, but the tone of the conversation had changed, voices were softer and topics more personal and as time continued to pass, she found herself becoming impatient. Her time was now severely limited for a reason she could not share, and if this was her one chance to feel something like this, it was slipping away by his over gentlemanly behaviour which was obstructing the possibility of it fulfilling its destiny.

She kissed him gently and as his lips brushed hers, she could feel her entire body stirring in anticipation.

His voice was a virtual whisper "Would you like to move into the back seat where it's more comfortable?"

At last, he had got the message, but she paused for a moment while she tried to compile a response to replace the one on her lips of "God yes!"

He mistook the hesitation

"I'm sorry. What was I thinking? I was just a bit carried away by the moment. Come on, I'll walk you to your car."

She got out of the car and immediately opened one of the back doors smiling at him mischievously.

"Really?" His voice was tentative

"Absolutely" She smiled. "I feel exactly the same, but I have never ever ......" He silenced her with his finger over her lips,

"I know"

She slid across the back seat to make room for him beside her. As he pulled her close the fullness of his stomach pressed against her through his ill-fitting tee shirt and his floppy unkempt hair fell into his eyes, but it was all adorable, refreshingly real, perfect. She knew she was about to cross a line she could not come back from, to cause damage that could never be repaired and although she was aware there may be consequences to bear, she had no idea of the deadly decision she was about to make.

Lovingly he unbuttoned her blouse and slid his hand onto her pounding heart. The touch of his hand on her skin felt like an honour, a long-awaited reward and as he caressed her naked flesh, she felt that she might die if he stopped. As his hands began to explore her body, she could feel her legs shaking and hoped he hadn't noticed. Her heart was racing, and her body perspiring and she wanted to stay in this moment forever. Tentatively but unashamedly, she caressed the growing outline through the fabric of his groin and the impact of her touch ignited a new urgency. The gentle softness of his hand was sending tremors through her as his fingers traced a tiny pattern from her knee to her inner thigh. Slowly he eased himself on top of her and she no longer cared where they were or who may notice for, to her, this was it, this was unstoppable, this was destiny, this was home.

This stranger was hers and she was his and nothing was going to stop it or spoil it. Not now. For the first time in her life, she felt she belonged in a man's arms. This chubby, arrogant, unkempt person had flicked a switch somewhere and she was locked in.

The distant seafront lights blurred out of focus and the sound of the traffic faded away as her senses became unable to absorb anything other than the outline of his face in the dusk, the sweet male animal scent of his body and the dulcet tones of his laboured breathing. As a curtain dropped between them and the outside world, nothing else existed. Caught in some pocket of existence outside of reason or responsibility nothing had ever felt so real, so powerful or so right. Gently he rocked her through level upon level of physical pleasure. Eyes maintained contact and hands remained clasped until their bodies shuddered in convulsion after convulsion of sexual pleasure. Finally, they fell apart exhausted, laying quietly whilst the pounding of their hearts started to subside.

The practicalities in the aftermath of lovemaking were usually a little awkward, even with Carl but here in the back seat of a stranger's car, in a pub car park, the most awkward and embarrassing situation she could think of there was none. They flowed out of lovemaking as easily as they had flowed into it and the conversation was as vibrant as before. She checked her phone again and noticed several more missed calls and also that it was now after midnight.

"I have to go." The smile on her face was uneasy.

"I know you do." She hoped he hadn't guessed she had a boyfriend, but she suspected that he had

She wanted to ask if she could see him again, but he had already taken her phone from her hand and sent himself a text. His own phone announced its arrival.

"There. Now I have you." If it was meant as a threat it was a welcome one because she so much wanted to be had by this wonderful creature who ticked none of the boxes she was supposed to be filling.

As she left the car and walked toward her own, she knew he was watching her and although she didn't look back, she was smiling. Starting the car, she acknowledged that all the feelings she should have, guilt, remorse, dread, the wedding and Carl were nowhere in sight. The only feeling she had was joy, her heart was dancing and the only thing of which she was certain was that she could not wait to see him again.

Carl was too full of apologies to question her on where she had been, assuming she had stayed out with friends to teach him a lesson. She didn't ask him for an explanation any more than she offered one herself. She simply threw her clothes into the wash basket and headed for a much-needed shower whilst assuring him that it didn't matter as she had celebrated with people from work.

She stood in the shower as the warm water ran down her body enjoying the solitude. She didn't want to break this spell and needed to relive every moment, recall every word, every touch in the privacy of this quiet secure space.

"I'm sorry Sophie." He yawned as he slid across the bed and nestled behind her gently pulling her back to him

"It's fine. Honestly." She said dismissively. She wanted him to be quiet while she continued to commit to memory every moment of what may turn out to be the best few hours of her entire life. These warm images lingered before carrying her into gentle slumber.

Chapter 4

The radio jump started her back to life after the best night's sleep she had enjoyed for weeks. Today butterflies had replaced the churning in her stomach, and instead of taking advantage of a few more moments in bed, she couldn't wait to start the day in anticipation of further contact with her new lover. She knew there were serious issues to be dealt with, if anything were to come of it, but for now she wanted nothing other than to enjoy it. Nothing else mattered today.

She found herself taking extra care over her hair and makeup and carefully selecting her outfit, paying extra care to pick out lacey, matching underwear, just in case.

She arrived at the office and booted up her PC staring expectantly at her phone. Willing it to ring or for a message to arrive. She made coffee, stamped and filed some invoices and checked her phone again. She hadn't told him when he could contact her, so she had made sure her phone was on silent during the night just in case he believed she was single. She wanted desperately to make that the truth before she had to confess to being a two-timing bitch. She checked the phone again but there had been no messages or missed calls. Not during the night and not this morning. She held it in her hand willing it to spring to life, but it remained dormant, silent and hostile.

Eventually she put it on the desk and took a pile of booking forms from her 'in tray'. Suddenly there it was, the long-awaited beep. Smiling from ear to ear, her heart pounding, she pressed the button to read it. It was from Carl! She cursed him several times for the disappointment and didn't even bother to read it.

"Are you ready then hotshot?" Tim looked rather agitated as he peered round her office door

"Ready for what?"

"Your presentation! Doooh." Tim ridiculed, leaving his mouth hanging open to enhance his impression of an idiot.

"Don't you think yesterdays was enough?" she was irritated at having to speak to anyone at all.

"What?" Tim looked bewildered, "you came in and did it on Sunday?"

Sophie froze for a moment trying to decide if Tim had finally lost his mind or if it was a pathetic attempt at a wind-up.

"Sophie, everyone is in the board room waiting!" Tim snapped, his eyes widening, in an effort to emphasize the urgency.

Quickly she checked her calendar on which she religiously marked off each day, but the weekend and Monday were still intact. She looked back at Tim for clarity.

"Wakey Wakey! It's Monday morning," he mocked, "have you finally lost it?"

Confusion overwhelmed her as her hands started to shake.

Through the window she could see a group of suited men peering expectantly in her direction but none of them, except Paul, looked familiar. She had no time to try to make sense of it, so she quickly snatched her presentation disc from her case where she thought she had packed it before going to the pub to celebrate, but now considering it was in there from packing it at home. None of the acetates had been printed so she loaded the sheets into the printer and tried to collect herself. It seemed to take forever to print them off and Tim swiftly abandoned her to make himself a drink whilst shaking his head condescendingly. Sophie's mind was spinning in some sort of loop as she scooped together the hot slides, pushed passed smiling Tim, and scurried in the direction of the meeting room.

How could this be Monday? What about the presentation she had already done? Her pay rise and ………….. What about HIM? Where did her new lover fit into this and why hadn't he contacted her?

Her hands were shaking as she loaded the first slide onto the projector, which was still warming up. Someone cleared their throat to grab her attention, the slide was upside down and as she quickly reached for it, it floated to the floor. She bent down to retrieve it feeling the pressure in her face from both embarrassment and gravity. She knew she was bright red as she slapped the offending item back on the hot glass plate. Someone cleared their throat again. It was back to front. She could feel her thin blouse clinging to the damp skin of her back as she made another attempt to correct the slide. The sexy straggly bits of hair she has purposely omitted from her bun were now plastered to her neck with sweat.

Repeatedly telling herself to calm down, had little effect as she fought off the tears that were building on the bridge of her nose, and the stifled sobs queuing in her throat. She must not break down. Tim would love that! She stuttered a few monotone sentences from the first slide, but she was reading the words, she was not presenting, just reading. It was all her jumbled brain could manage. She reached for the next slide, but it didn't make any sense, even to her. Yesterday she had introduced this slide with some compelling examples, but she couldn't remember what they were, it didn't seem to follow the last one. The slides were out of order and she had no idea which one came next. She tried to think, she couldn't think. She looked up at the bewildered faces before her, trying to decide if she should apologise, ask for time to compose herself or run out of the room.

She tried to continue with a few random sentences she could remember from her rehearsals at home, but her sub conscious was shouting at her 'this is a disaster' she already knew it. She saw the frowns and raised eyebrows around the table but was powerless to redeem the situation. Her sodden blouse now sucked onto her skin and was almost transparent. She needed to get this over with. She needed to think but this damn presentation was in the way. Talking ten to the dozen and pushing one slide after the other hoping it meant more to her audience than the sequence of words meant to her, she eventually thanked them with equal disparity and headed out of the room without allowing time for questions or feedback. The only sensible question would be "what the hell are you talking about" and she didn't need to hear that.

Back at her desk, she slumped in her chair and tried to assess her sanity in the peace and quiet of her own space.

Tim followed after a few moments and sat at his own desk with the same astonished expression as before and then asked her something she didn't answer or even hear. She checked her phone again, checked the calendar again, and sat in her torturous void. She knew what a dream felt like and this had not been a dream. This had a been a day like any other. No disjointed events, no random images, she had lived Monday and she had met the only man who had touched her soul. She needed some air.

"I don't feel well Tim. Tell everyone I've gone home sick"

Tim nodded uncomfortably and made no further effort to speak to her, but she knew he would be blabbing this over the entire hotel the moment she was out of the way.

She snatched her coat from the hanger and ran out of the office, stumbling over the carpark in high heels until she reached the sanctuary of her car. For a moment she did nothing. She gripped the steering wheel as though using it to keep her balance, as she stared through the windscreen totally emotionless for several minutes. Suddenly, worrying that someone may follow her out of the office to check on her, she started the engine and drove along the sea front with no plan in mind other than to make some sense of what had just happened. Parking outside the newsagent, she rushed in to buy a daily paper. The date was Monday.

Slumping back on the driver's seat, she relayed the facts to herself out loud. There had been no pay rise and Carl had not stood her up which means there was no encounter with her lover. The fear for her sanity was secondary. She had waited her entire life for something that had suddenly and miraculously felt within her reach and now it had been snuffed out by the damp fingers of reality. There could be no doubt that it had been nothing more than a fantasy of her own creation. She walked along the beach still watching her phone. She recalled the text he had sent from her phone to his and quickly checked her sent messages looking for an unknown number but there was none.

She sat down on the damp sand with her back to a rock and watched the never-ending grey waves glide over each other and return dutifully to the ocean. The perspiration was now stale on her face and body, making her feel dirty and drab. Her dark hair hung limply from an unravelling bun and her face itched where the sweat, foundation and tears had mixed together and reset in a crust under her eyes. She sat wallowing in her misery and filth until darkness fell at around five when she forced herself up onto scratched salt stung legs, one hold up had slid to her knee so she removed her shoes and stepped out of it without bothering to pick it up. As she carried her high heels back to the steps on freezing bare feet, the tears started to well up again, adding new warmth and moisture to the crusty mess on her face.

Luckily, she was the first to enter the flat which allowed her a few minutes to splash water on her face, detangle the matt of hair at her nape and slip on a tracksuit and warm socks. By the time Carl breezed in, things appeared normal as she peeled the potatoes with the TV in the background.

She looked at him in an appraising way, slim, muscular, trendy, sporty Carl, and yet her heart was the heaviest it had ever felt. The man who brought her to life, her sparkly eyed, chubby, unfashionable guy had gone. Even though he had never existed, she remembered him, his scent, his touch, his voice, his laugh and as she placed the peeled potatoes into the pan grief overwhelmed her, it felt like he had died. She had been touched by the suggestion of true love, tasted it, held it, been captured by it and now it was gone, and the loss was unbearable.

She threw the peelings into the bin and walked quietly to the door as Carl laughed at some slapstick comedy show. Calmly she walked into the bathroom, locked the door, sat on the floor with her knees pulled to her chest and sobbed.

Chapter 5

The night felt endless. Sophie lay silently staring into the darkness, listening to Carl breathing as he rested in carefree slumber. She envied him. Trying to find some logical explanation for the last 24 hours occupied every available space in her head and exhausted every cell of brainpower. She acknowledged that she was in shock and when a person is in shock their ability to process information is impaired, but there seemed to be nothing impaired about her detailed recollection of her hours with her nameless lover. Could it really have been nothing more than her imagination, a dream that had been created from within her own mind? She went over it again. She had certainly had dreams that felt real before but there was always something about them that separated them from reality, something that prevents everyone from running around, mixing dream memories with real ones. This dream was just too complete and too detailed and there were no random interjections or loss of credibility about it. She didn't just see it, she felt it, tasted it and had fallen in love. This ghost of her own invention had shown her what love felt like.

Whatever it was, it had changed her, and now she couldn't determine what impact this had on her plans or what impact it was meant to have. If it was a glimpse of what could be then she should leave Carl immediately and just hope to find it someday or perhaps it was a warning that moments such as those exist only in dreams – in the imagination – the only place where love is perfect.

Compelling as these questions were, there was nothing more compelling at this moment than the heartbreak of the loss of her soul mate, the man who completed her and whom she had lost so cruelly before sharing the wonderful things that may have been in store for them. Telling herself over and over that he doesn't exist didn't help to erase the memory of him or his presence which she still felt all around her. She wondered if she would spend the rest of her life trying to find him again. Spend her days chasing a ghost with this ache that gripped her chest until she could barely breathe.

She was still replaying the same questions and conversations in her head like a stuck record when the alarm announced the end of her window of opportunity to gain some sleep. Without sleep work was going to be a challenge. She took a shower and made herself a very strong coffee instead of her usual cup of tea.

Quietly she placed Carl's tea on the table beside him, hoping not to wake him because she didn't feel capable of a conversation, not even an exchange of pleasantries. In fact, she didn't want to speak to anyone at all. She would wake him on her way out. There was no room in her head for anything today other than to quieten her thoughts and to settle this turmoil in her stomach which far surpassed the morning turmoil she had become accustomed to. By comparison she reflected that a few days ago she had been happy. She hadn't felt happy, but in comparison to this crushing grief she realised she had been enviably content.

She left without waking Carl, deciding that it was time he stopped relying on her as his mother, and as she sat behind the steering wheel gathering the motivation to drive to work, she replaced her misery with determination. She was not a religious person, yet she found herself pleading to whatever divine being might be listening, to take pity on her aching heart. "Please, I just want him back" She was not going to roll over and accept what had happened, she was going to solve it. There had to be some explanation and if it wasn't her sanity in question then maybe some scientific or supernatural one. She wasn't going to give up but deep down she knew this was desperation talking, denial in its strongest form, but for now it was a lifeline, and she would hold onto it a while longer.

As she drove the familiar journey, she heard her phone announce a text message which she knew would be Carl asking why she hadn't woken him. She parked the car and blinked the tears from her eyes as she opened the message whilst trying to think of a plausible excuse, but the message was from an unknown number.

"Hi. Hope you got home ok?"

Time stood still for a moment. She knew immediately that it was him! There was no doubt. She didn't know how or why from half a dozen words, but she knew. Her hands were shaking as she replied, muttering thanks to a God she didn't believe in for answering her plea. Frantically she typed as though trying to hook him like a fish before he escaped again.

"Yes. Thanks. How are you?"

"I'm good. Well except for the fact that I just can't seem to stop thinking about you and I was hoping we could meet again. That is if you want to?"

"Want to?" She thought, if only he knew! Her hands busied again.

"Yes, that would be lovely. I've been thinking of you too."

"Do you want to have lunch today?"

"Yes, that would be great."

The messages passed back and forth until she was a full half hour late for work, but she didn't care because this miracle was more important than her career, and when she eventually skipped into the office it was with a smile on her face. Her whole being had been invigorated with anticipation of her lunch date and the prospect of seeing her man once again. She could call him this without hesitation – he belonged to her and she wanted more than anything to show him she was his. She no longer cared about the stupid presentation one bit.

Tim noticed her change of mood immediately. Geeky, skinny dull Tim actually noticed something for once.

"You look happy. Trying to work out what to do with the extra cash?"

"What cash?"

"Your pay rise of course." His tone was a mix of humour and resentment, but she didn't notice because she was far too disturbed by the inference.

"Something like that." She said as she sat down at her desk and checked her diary. It was Tuesday and she wasn't sure that she expected anything else, but if she had been given a pay rise then this meant the presentation went well and............ She shook her head as though trying to settle her thoughts back into order.

Was she back in the dream? Was any of this real? It felt real and Tim looked real and everything seemed as it should be.

She tried to concentrate on her work which was as normal and uneventful as any other day, and although she had one eye on the clock, urging the hands to transport her to lunchtime, she had an uneasiness about the reality of this date. Though nervous and uncontrollably excited, a tiny niggle in the back of her mind was contemplating that she may still be sleeping beside Carl.

As she entered the bar, she looked for him in the same place as before, but the stools were taken by a group of young men.

Her heart was pounding for a million reasons, none of which made any sense, but she needed to know if this was ever real. As she made her way across the room a hand reached out and caught hers. She didn't need to turn around, she could feel his presence.

"Hi."

"Hi yourself." She smiled as he pulled her towards him

"I haven't been able to think of anything else since last night," he confessed "but I don't think that's a sensible thing to say to a lady who might use this power to make my life a misery." There was a sense of fun in his voice.

"Your secret is safe with me." She smiled as she kissed him gently on the lips.

She tried to put all her doubts about the reality of the situation to the back of her mind along with the fear of her insanity, a fear which had been growing by the hour throughout the morning. Here was the one person she could confide in yet how on earth could she ask him...

"Excuse me but are you a figment of my imagination?" It was laughable. He would run for the hills and she wouldn't blame him.

"Penny for them?" His mischievous eyes became a little more serious in concern for the expression he was seeing on her face.

"Oh, it's nothing."

"It doesn't look like nothing."

"I just can't believe this, this thing between us." It wasn't a lie, but it was not exactly what she had been thinking at that moment.

She knew she needed to shake out of this as he was reading her like a book but somehow, she couldn't deceive him and didn't want to try

"I'm sorry it's just that all this seems so fast and confusing. I have a fiancé and ...."

He put his finger on her lips to silence her and held her close. All the questions she wanted to ask, and all the doubts which had crowded her head, melted away as his embrace convinced her that everything was going to be alright.

They ordered sandwiches one with fries and one with salad but then decided they both wanted half of what the other had and as they clumsily passed food between plates, she found this comical, sloppy sharing of food hilarious. Carl would never do anything like this. He was far too concerned about what others might think. Far too aware of his surroundings, whereas right now she was experiencing the thrill of two people who had become totally unaware of anything or anyone other than each other.

They kissed more passionately as they said goodbye to return to work. Sophie didn't know what this was, or where it might lead, but it didn't matter. All that mattered was that he had returned to her life and had promised to text her, and that meant she would see him again.

"I don't even know your name."

"It's John."

"So, John, are you married?" She tried to sound light-hearted as she rocked playfully against him.

"No."

"Girlfriend?"

"Maybe I do now?" It was the perfect answer

She hugged his ample waist and he tapped it comically.

"I need to lose a few pounds."

"No," she snapped "you are perfect. I don't want you any other way – ever."

"Ever? Are we planning ever?"

"Hmmm – maybe"

"Well I'm not scared of forever." He grinned.

"Me neither."

"Go on – you'll be late." He said as he gently let go of her hand.

Once again, she could feel him watching her as she made her way to her car in her high heels and very restrictive pencil skirt. She felt good and sexy and she knew without looking back that he was thinking the same thing.

As she started the engine, she checked her rear-view mirror. He was still watching but fear was starting to replace euphoria. Was she about to drive away, leaving him in a place she might never find him again? She slowed the car, he waived, she had no excuse to stay so slowly she crept out of the carpark and turned onto the road. She swallowed hard and muttered another prayer.

The afternoon was punctuated with regular messages from John. Her prayer had been heard! She was so captivated by the exchanges that she was furious when a message from Carl interrupted the flow. She sent him a curt response and hoped he would take the hint.

Among the messages, she had promised to sort out her relationship with Carl and suddenly this didn't seem such a big deal to her. In fact, she couldn't wait to get him out of her life so she could have the freedom to see John full time. Carl would find someone else easily enough and she didn't feel an ounce of jealousy at the thought of it. That surely told her everything.

Rationalising the horrific presentation day became suddenly and conveniently easy. It was obvious that it was the awful day that had been a bad dream, a nightmare and now thankfully she was back in reality. She couldn't have been happier and even the task of cancelling her wedding seemed like a minor hurdle, an irritating inconvenience.

"Good day babe?" Carl was as cheerful and affectionate as ever and she was a little taken aback by a rush of guilt which, up until that point had been suppressed by sheer exuberance.

"Good thanks." She tried to keep her tone practical and barely polite so as not to give him reason to feel everything was fine, it felt deceitful and misleading to show him any affection.

"You ok?"

"Just tired." She lied. Buying herself time to think, and to plan her exit in the most painless way possible. She decided it was kinder not to tell Carl she had met someone else.

She watched him tossing the stir fry, which was his Tuesday night signature dish, and noticed how attractive he really was. His face rugged but in an almost pretty way, his torso toned and muscular, his unusual chocolate brown hair sexily ruffled and his buttocks were firm, rounded and pert in his tight jeans. He would have no problem in finding someone soon – she was sure of it.

What was even stranger, was that now her decision to leave him had been made, she found a new fondness for him, a fondness which had likely been thwarted by the resentment of feeling trapped.

She didn't want to hurt him, but she knew it was inevitable that he would be the collateral damage of her new adventure. Staying out of obligation or sympathy, was not an option, she just needed a way of starting the conversation which would ignite the flames. She would then be able to fan them a little as she watched their relationship turn to ashes. She decided that attack was the easiest route, to move the blame onto him if she could think of something.

She put on her serious face and pretended to be deep in thought.

"What is it?" He was immediately concerned which made her feel even worse, but she had to create some friction.

"Should we really be making such a big commitment to each other Carl?"

He was visibly shocked.

"What? Why?"

"Well it was only this new year when we had all that fuss over the girl from work. You know the one you kissed at midnight."

Carl was looking totally bewildered

"What? We are not going to go over all that again surely?" She could see his heart sink as he sighed, the way he had done many times when she had brought this up.

"It was a New Year kiss. It meant nothing. It was the bloody millennium, everyone was kissing! You said you were ok with it now."

"I thought I was, but I guess I'm not."

"What more do you want me to say? To do? Leave my job?"

"No! Maybe it's me you should be leaving not your job?"

"What?" He looked distraught.

"If you can feel attracted to someone else, then maybe I'm just not the one?" She knew she was being pathetic.

"Where has all this come from? Have you been talking to Niki again?"

"No. I just think that if two people are truly in love, in love enough to be getting married then they just shouldn't be feeling attracted to anyone else or kissing anyone else."

He walked over to her and pulled her gently into his arms.

"I am not attracted to anyone else. You are my girl. I only want you and if I could wind back time and maybe have a few less beers, she wouldn't have got a look in."

Suddenly the words spoken by Kelly came into her head – why would you want a love that made you feel so wretched – and she wondered if that kind of love could make a person act wretchedly too, for she felt a certain self-loathing at what she was doing to her adoring Carl, on account of a flirtation with a man she hardly knew.

"You are my gir,l" he buried his head soulfully in her hair, "am I still your guy?"

She didn't answer.

"Hey," he lifted her face up to meet his and smiled affectionately, "am I still your guy?"

She nodded and hugged him gently as her heart sank lower and lower.

She served up the stir fry and noticed how often he glanced her way for reassurance. She had clearly planted some doubts in his mind, and she was sure he was going to work harder and harder to keep her, which did not fit her plan at all.

She wanted to blame him. She wanted to be the victim here. She didn't want to shoulder the blame for breaking his heart but what she was doing wasn't fair and she knew it. She thought long and hard about how on earth she was going to approach this again. She couldn't let this drag on until cancelling the wedding resulted in catastrophic financial loss for her parents.

Time was running out and she was annoyed at her false start. She couldn't leave it!

"I'm not happy Carl." The words left her mouth almost without her permission, catapulted from sheer desperation as she sat down at the table. She had said them a few times in her head, and then, wham - they were out there.

Carl did not want to face this, his expression said it all. He sensed the gravity of his situation and reverted immediately to begging.

"Please baby. Please don't say that!" He was already on his knees holding both of her hands in his.

"Whatever it is I can fix it! We can fix it ... together."

"No, we can't!" The tears were flowing freely down her cheeks as she tried to console this lovely person who had played such an important role in her life.

"Why? Why can't we?"

"Because I don't think I am in love with you."

"I know that you are. It's just last-minute doubts." His voice was desperate but tainted with an element of the inevitable.

She shook her head still crying and pulled her long dark hair back into an imaginary elastic band.

"Is there?" he almost choked on the words, "is there someone else?"

She felt his agony through his trembling hands as he awaited her reply

"No. No, of course not!" She just couldn't hurt him any more

"Then we will get through this," he kissed her wet face "I love you enough for both of us."

She kissed him back gently and went to bed without touching her meal. He stayed for a while staring at the TV and poking the food around his plate. The TV screen was just a series of images making no sense to him, telling no story, he sat and stared without seeing it and eventually Sophie felt the weight of him lay down beside her.

She remained still and silent so as not to engage in further discussion as she closed her eyes and tried to block out the images of Carl's heartbroken face. How could something so wonderful bring so much misery? She felt no relief at having started the ball rolling, instead only the terrible worry that Carl might never recover from what she was doing to him.

She felt him turn away from her to sleep, which was something he had never done before, and she noticed how cold the gap between their backs was. Cold and empty.

She pondered the question of when is one person's happiness worth another person's heartbreak? Never?

Chapter 6

In the morning it seemed he had totally forgotten their fight, as he had done so many times before. Once again, he had reverted back to status quo, and pure habit had drawn him to his usual position, nestled behind her with his arm around her waist. Gently she tried to move it before he woke up, but it was too late.

She tried to push his arm away, but he held fast

"Carl, I need to be out of the door in half an hour!" she snapped

"Stay here a bit longer ... I think I know something we can do in fifteen minutes."

She couldn't believe he was being so blatant in view of her revelation, and his arrogance angered her.

"Did you hear nothing I said last night?"

"You were very quiet and a bit down last night but I don't think you told me why?" He sounded genuinely puzzled as he propped his dishevelled head up on his elbow.

"Are you joking?"

"No, but you were ages in the bathroom. Were you not well?

"Bathroom? I wasn't ages in the bathroom I went to bed before you!"

"Whatever." Carl couldn't be bothered to argue over something so trivial. Sophie on the other hand, had her own reasons for clarifying the detail.

"What did we have for dinner last night?" She frowned

"Can't you remember?" He laughed.

"Yes," she said confidently, "stir fry."

Carl laughed again. "I think you need to get your head checked lover."

Sophie's heart stopped once again. Surely not again. This can't be happening again.

"It's Wednesday today, right?"

"No babe, it's Tuesday today."

Sophie, with eyes fixed firmly forward, walked calmly and silently to the bathroom and turned on the shower. Her head was spinning, her heart pounding ... if this is Tuesday then the Tuesday with John didn't happen. She felt sick. Sick and terrified. Was she truly insane? Ill? Deluded? The ache in the pit of her stomach was surpassed only by the ache in her heart. She put her hands against the wall and vomited violently into the flow of the shower.

She arrived at the office with no recollection at all of leaving the shower cubicle or driving to work. Tim didn't mention her pay rise that day, but she knew he wouldn't because he was the wrong Tim just as this was the wrong office the wrong day and the wrong world.

She checked her phone for the messages from John and the ones she had sent back to him but there were none. She knew there would be none just as there had been no divine intervention into her misery. She looked for his number, but it wasn't on her call list. She tried to remember it, to visualise the number sequence in the hope that dialling it might restore him to her real life, but no numbers seemed familiar. Staring blankly at the pile of unprocessed papers mounting on her 'in tray' was serving no purpose other than to cause her to accept the possibility that her mental health was the issue.

She sent a desperate text to Niki to meet her at lunchtime without any explanation and as she arrived at the café Nicki was already seated with two cups of coffee on the table. Niki looked up at her sympathetically, assuming she had decided to cancel her wedding plans. She had tried to practise her response on the way and decided she would not try to dissuade her from her plan to leave Carl. The two women looked at one another for a few seconds before Sophie slumped into the chair and opened the conversation on a shockingly different subject.

"I think I am going insane."

Niki smiled momentarily, believing Sophie was referring to something stupid or forgetful she had done, but the fear in her eyes caused Niki's smile to drop into a solemn stare as Sophie blurted out the events of the past two days randomly. A conglomerate of events strung together between sobs. Of duplicated, conflicting days, meetings and texts, presentations, sex, love and despair. Sophie's account was so incredible, so ridiculous that Niki couldn't decide on how to handle her. She clearly was in need of some sort of medical intervention but, on her own admission, she seemed to know that already.

"So, let me sum this up," Niki tried to resound it back in the hope Sophie would laugh at herself, "you have met and fallen in love with a man. You have seen him twice, but you now think it was a fantasy? Don't you think the timing of this is a bit of a coincidence following our conversation on Friday?"

"Yes, I do, and I've been thinking exactly the same thing, but that doesn't mean it didn't happen to me."

"I think it's more likely that you have stress than some mental illness Sophie, but I do think you should see a doctor. The mind can be very powerful when it is pushed to its limit."

Her words were reassuring but her tone certainly wasn't, and Sophie knew that her friend was trying to handle her with the condescending voice of negotiation used for talking down a maniac brandishing a knife.

The two friends looked at each other for a moment before Sophie tried to alleviate the tension with spontaneous laughter.

"I am pathetic, aren't I?" she laughed wishing she had kept the whole thing to herself.

"No. You just fell in love with an idea and now you are disappointed that it wasn't real."

"Yes, that's it. Thanks, Nik" she said quickly, grateful to latch onto any rational explanation on offer.

"What for?"

"For listening and not thinking I'm mad!" Sophie said quietly with a hint of sarcasm

"I do think you are mad," she corrected laughing awkwardly, "but aren't we all a little bit?"

They parted and Sophie returned to work feeling a little stupid, a little let down but also a little relieved. Hearing it repeated to her out loud had interjected some common sense. So, the love of her life didn't exist but at least she had not broken Carl's heart, and her life wasn't so bad compared to most. She would put it all behind her and focus on the wedding plans.

For the first hour she continued to feel the relief. The newly restored contentment and the gratitude that she had been given a second chance to appreciate what she had. Even though she had messed up her immediate career prospects, she had a gorgeous, devoted man who couldn't wait to become her husband.

She authorised invoices, confirmed bookings and allocated function rooms but as the afternoon went on, she could feel holes developing in this newly woven veil of concealment. Her heart was already burning through the façade of contentment.

Holes opening like tiny sores and no amount of self-lecturing could heal them. Fantasy or not, this man was under her skin and she feared she may spend the rest of her life in love with a shadow. She may as well have fallen in love with a character from a movie.

It was stir-fry for dinner, just as she had expected, and after clearing away the plates she sat cuddled up to Carl for a while, trying her best to feel something. She kissed him in the hope that it would stir something deep inside her, told him she loved him in the hope that hearing the words would make it true, stroked his face in the hope that desire would take over. It didn't. Instead, she was watching the clock and urging the minutes to pass more quickly, for the evening to end and the night to begin. She couldn't get the idea out of her head that there was some possibility that sleep may reunite her with John, even if he wasn't real, even if he could never be a part of her reality, she was still excited at the prospect of seeing him in her dreams.

As she disentangled herself from Carl's limp arms, she pushed gently against his toned torso to free herself, but his fingers lingered lovingly on hers until the growing distance between them caused his hand to fall dejectedly. She smiled apologetically and yawned deeply in way of an explanation. Inside she was feeling guilty and disloyal as she sneaked away from her trusting boyfriend in the hope of meeting her fantasy lover.

She went to bed and tried to sleep but after an hour of counting sheep, singing in her head, trying to empty her head, deep breathing and 'trying to find her centre' (whatever that was) she was still wide awake when Carl jumped in beside her and pulled her close. She pretended to be asleep as she didn't want him to keep her awake even longer, but within minutes she was furious at hearing him snoring soundly while she was still wide awake.

She went into the kitchen and poured herself a large whisky and swallowed a couple of sleeping pills but an hour later she was still staring at the clock and willing sleep to descend on her. Her frustration turned to anger as she punched the pillow and then her head for refusing to sleep. She needed to calm down, she needed to relax. She pondered that no one ever really remembers the actual moment they fall asleep, so it could happen at any moment, she lay, she sighed, and she waited.

The room suddenly lit up, but Carl was too deep in sleep to notice. Damn it, it was coming from her phone and she suspected it was telling her it was fully charged. She picked it up to unplug it and saw the new message sign on the screen with the name John. Her throat closed and she felt the perspiration instantly on her chest. Had she fallen asleep without realising? Was this now a dream? She was sure she hadn't, but she turned to Carl to check. He was still snoring. She checked that he looked exactly the same as he had when he went to bed, everything looked right. Gently she pressed the open button on her phone.

"Can you meet me? Now?"

She was typing frantically.

"Yes, where?"

"Sea front. Outside the pub."

"Ok."

She was out of bed in an instant and pulling on her jeans. She quietly picked up her top and then wondered if it really mattered if she woke Carl or not. If this was only a dream why did she care? But she didn't want him to stop her, even if he wasn't real so quietly, she sneaked out of the flat and didn't put her shoes on until she was on the steps outside.

As she crossed the road to the promenade, she glanced quickly along in the direction of the pub and there standing beside a bench was that familiar and wonderful silhouette she had been longing to see. The closer she got the higher her spirit soared until a few strides away from him she had to stop for a second to savour the moment.

"Hi." How could the tone of one word convey so much?

"Hi." She returned the greeting in an identical way. The mood was set. No questions were asked, and no explanations given as he offered his hand. She took it. Perfect.

They walked in silence for a while. Silence that was neither awkward nor hostile. Neither inattentive nor empty. Silence that provided the perfect moment of silence for him to break.

"I think I love you."

"Don't say that!" She laughed dismissively.

"I just had to see you. I don't know what this thing is but it's quite something. I really do think it might be love you know," he smiled raising his eyebrows comically, "never felt it before."

She left the silence hanging for a moment before breaking into a grin and responding.

"Nor me. Actually, I think I love you too."

In the background, doubts about the reality of this moment chatted relentlessly in her head – reminding her that his declaration of love was probably also of her own making. His words were most likely another addition to her perfect fantasy, but she didn't care. Real or not, she was going to enjoy the thrill of it.

They walked down onto the sand and sat on the rocks and suddenly the air didn't feel so cold and she thought perhaps she had fixed the temperature in her fantasy too.

If so, then isn't it better to dispel it all right now? Perhaps she should confront this while she is still in it? She took a deep breath and started to parade her insanity before him.

"Sometimes I feel like this isn't real. Like we are in a dream or something."

"Too good to be true, am I?" He laughed.

"Seriously," she continued, trying to project a note of concern "I know this sounds crazy but some days I have woken up and your number has disappeared from my phone."

"Maybe your boyfriend deleted me?" He suggested making a playfully frightened face.

"There's more. The day he didn't turn up at the pub after I got a pay rise everyone denied that it happened and ..." she stopped herself as she watched his face change.

"Maybe you dreamt it didn't happen?" He looked concerned in his attempt to invent a possible explanation. Gratefully she decided to take the escape he was offering.

"Probably. I think I am a bit stressed."

He took the self-diagnosis as an invitation to fix her, as he pulled her into his arms onto the damp sand.

"I know a perfect destressing activity."

Surely, they couldn't make love on the wet sand on a cold January night? It was a fleeting rhetorical question which did nothing to deter her from tugging urgently at his clothes, in an attempt to unite their bodies once again.

Giggling like children they rolled over and over gathering clumps of sand on their clothes until they came to rest against another cluster of rocks. Harshly but playfully, he tugged off her jeans, before unzipping his own and throwing himself clumsily on top of her. She squealed in surprise as he caught her wrists and held her arms firmly above her head kissing her deeply. She wriggled for a moment as though trying to free herself from capture, but she was already captured by his kiss, and had no desire to wriggle free for at least another century.

As he lowered his weight onto her, she could hear the power of the winter waves and feel the harshness of the stones grazing her legs. Each thrust delivered a delicious blend of pain and pleasure. Body and soul perfectly blended as they climbed rhythmically towards that ultimate climax, warmly cocooned from the icy air.

Her remaining clothes clung to her with perspiration which was snatched by the cold wind as quickly as it formed. The clammy hot cold sensations normally cringingly unpleasant stoked the fire of excitement already burning fiercely as she arched her body against him.

He grunted with each thrust and already she was feeling the onset of that familiar light-headedness - the wonderful intoxication telling her that an orgasm was only moments away.

As her body shuddered and then relaxed, her post orgasm sensitive skin became painfully aware of the rhythmic grazing of her legs and buttocks against the sharp rocks beneath her. It was the sweetest of discomfort until she felt the sequence of his convulsions and his body weight fall upon her, welding his skin to hers in sweat, salt water and sand. She picked off the strand of hair pasted to her face with sweat and smiled widely.

"Get off. You are crushing me!" She laughed.

Immediately he rolled away but didn't yet have the capacity to speak.

As his breathing slowed and their heartbeats subsided, the night air infiltrated their warm aura. Body heat was no longer radiating between them, and the cold felt even colder as it rushed into every space between their bodies like a winter wind through sparse bare trees.

"You hungry?" He eventually gasped blowing his breath into his hands.

"I'm freezing," she frowned "but yes I'm also starving."

"Come on." He was pulling her to her feet, already feeling for her jeans in the darkness. He handed them to her and began the search for his own. They hopped between legs using shoulders for support as they attempted to wriggle into jeans and wriggle feet back into damp shoes filled with sand.

His gritty hand took hers as he tugged her into a running pace up the steps, dragging her a few hundred yards up a side-street before slowing to a walking pace to catch his breath.

"I don't think there's anywhere open." She gasped between breaths, noting that he could run quite fast for a man of his build.

"There's a truckers café just off the roundabout." He pointed to a roadside cabin from which a welcoming light was shining. As they entered the warm café they were abruptly illuminated and evidence of their beach romp was embarrassingly obvious. Sand was still falling onto the tiled floor from stained clothes which were barely fastened, and their faces still flushed from the frenzied encounter. He laughed at her horrified expression as he picked up a tray and frowned at the labels on the sandwiches from the shelf, picking two up without even asking her.

"There we go. Ham and Beef."

His childlike bad manners were startling but strangely comforting. This lack of gentlemanly politeness felt warm and refreshingly decisive, almost as familiar as if she were his wife rather than a new girlfriend.

He grinned as she raised her eyebrows. She was falling in deeper and deeper.

He paid for the sandwiches and two hot chocolates, again without asking, took a knife and chose the table. Quickly he cut each of the rolls in half and swapped each half to make two rolls of mixed fillings. He looked happy and engrossed, proud of the spoils he had provided.

"Cut and shut." He said proudly

She frowned.

"It's a car-dealing phrase for two cars that have been...."

"Yes, I know what a cut and shut is" she interrupted being careful not to relate this to her mechanic fiancé, "I'm just wondering if I am destined to get a mish mash every time we eat."

"Shut up and come here," he chuckled "best of both worlds, what's not to like?"

As he leaned in and kissed her, she felt uneasy about his comment. The best of both worlds? Had that thought come from her? She kissed him back and then asked the cashier if she could borrow a pen. Taking a napkin, she started to write down the type of information she couldn't remember.

"What you up to?" he laughed.

"Just want a few details." She smiled and proceeded to ask him for the basics like his full name, his parents address in Filey and the name of the bank he worked for in London, also the registration number of his car. She then copied his phone number from the text message exchanges. She had no idea how this would help because if this wasn't real then the napkin would vanish along with everything else but still, she frantically scribbled on the annoyingly fragile napkin.

"Am I under arrest?" He joked.

"Am I acting like a stalker?" She sighed.

"Darling you can stalk me anytime," he kissed her on the forehead and wiped some of the remaining sand from her face, "Sophie?"

"Yes?"

"I do love you."

She closed her eyes to soak up the moment. That moment she had only imagined, was suddenly, actually hers. She didn't care what happened next because she had finally felt it and nothing could take this moment away from her, not ever.

"I love you too." She stroked his hand gently

"I will break up with Carl tomorrow." She spoke the words knowing that the chances were that tomorrow John would be gone as she resumed her life, but for now the promise was from her heart.

An hour later she was fumbling with the key and trying to decide if she should shower before getting into bed but if this was all a dream then did it really matter? She got quietly into bed beside Carl who was still soundly asleep, still oblivious that there was anything to worry about but firmly she held onto her napkin, as though keeping it in her fist while she slept would provide a handle by which she could hold onto her other world.

The alarm clock sounded, and she opened her eyes, fighting with the darkness to focus on something, anything to give her a clue. She slowly unfolded her fist under the duvet and, as expected, the napkin was gone. No telephone numbers to try, no addresses to check, nothing remained of her adventure or her lover.

Closing her eyes tightly she tried to remember anything she had written down, but Carl was stirring beside her and the glow of his bedside lamp was interrupting her concentration. Irritably she turned away from him and tried to concentrate

"What the..............................?" Carl screamed

Quickly she sat up and followed the direction of his stare to the sight before him. White sheets covered in sand and dirt on which were sprawled her bruised dirty and bleeding legs.

Chapter 7

Sophie felt every pore tingle. Beads of sweat began to form over her entire body as she tried frantically to think of a plausible explanation. Of course, the truth would have given her the release she so desperately sought but Carl's tortured expression was urging her not to destroy him so brutally. His eyes were searching hers for some reason to believe everything would be alright, and she knew she had to appease him, at least for now until she could do this more delicately, more humanly and in a way that would leave him with some respect for her.

"I couldn't sleep last night and went out for a walk to think"

She had no idea if this was the Carl she had cuddled up to last night or the one on whom she had turned her back after their argument.

For a moment, his face softened slightly in recognition that there may still be hope, but the change was only fleeting before his eyes narrowed in suspicion and his face tensed in anger.

"Sophie. Don't lie to me!" he screamed "I can fuckin' smell him on you!" His whole body was shaking as he tried to fight the tears and she could feel this physical pain almost as intensely as he.

"You said there was no-one else. You said you were still my girl. You're a damn liar!"

In his hand she could see a napkin. A crumpled napkin stained with the ink from her handwriting.

She realised she must have fallen asleep before the text from John. This was the Carl she had turned her back on.

"I....."she stammered; her mascara stained cheeks suddenly starkly pale, in contrast to the teary smudges.

"Just don't say anything!" he was almost hysterical, "I don't need to hear it."

His nose was running as tears trickled down his cheeks causing the fluids to pool around his mouth. He made no attempt to wipe it, as he held onto the dresser with both hands, as though unable to stand without support.

Quickly, Sophie jumped out of bed and pulled her jeans back on, hurriedly making her way to the door as she pulled her sweatshirt over her head and flicked her tangled hair out of the neck. She had no idea where she was going, other than away from here, away from this whole situation and the devastation she had caused. As she fumbled with her trainers, he ran out of the room and snatched her car keys from the hook by the door.

"You are not going anywhere!" His anger had returned as he stood fast in her path

"Just let me go Carl."

"To run to him? No, I won't. You are staying here 'til we sort this out"

"There is nothing to sort out." She said gently as she put her hand on his chest to push him aside.

He yielded, flopping limply against the wall in his surrender to let her walk by but he held on firmly to her keys. Without her keys she couldn't go far, and he knew it, but she didn't care as she ran down the stairs into the street. She kept running through the cold morning mist with no idea where she was heading or even what time it was. Day was breaking so she assumed it was around 7.30 and she ought to be getting ready for work, but instead she found herself leaning against a crumbling backstreet wall, gasping for breath and trying to decide where to go. She was dirty. Unwashed without underwear. Lank strands of dirty hair framed her salty, gritty face, mascara stained tears streaking from puffy red eyes. Her mouth was dry from running and she could smell the staleness of her breath and feel the disgusting film covering her unbrushed teeth. She pushed herself off the wall and walked to the taxi rank to take a cab to Niki's house.

Niki was almost ready for work when she opened the door and gasped.

"Sophie! What on earth has happened?"

Over Niki's shoulder she could see Pete drinking coffee in the kitchen.

"Come in" Niki pulled her friend bodily from the street.

"Can you lend me some money for the taxi?" she blurted

Niki obediently handed her purse over without question and Sophie rushed out of the house and back in again, interrupting an exchange of raised eyebrows between her two hosts.

Even so, she felt comforted by the familiar surroundings of her sanctuary from Carl's wrath.

The house Niki shared with Pete was just a modest terrace, but it was tastefully decorated and the kitchen where Pete stood beside the breakfast bar was colourful and trendy. Niki flicked on the bright red kettle and popped a couple of slices of bread into the matching toaster while beckoning Sophie to sit on a bar stool to be waited on.

Pete seemed to realise this was no time for him to be eavesdropping and kissed his girlfriend a hurried goodbye, raising his eyebrows again as he grabbed his jacket (which was more suitable for a man twice his age) and made good his escape. Pete was the most average man Sophie could imagine. There was nothing exceptional about him in either looks or personality, still Niki seemed content with her lot, but it remained a mystery to Sophie. Of the three women, Niki was definitely 'the looker'. Kelly was very eye-catching but most of her was bleach, makeup and skin-tight clothing, Sophie was pretty enough in a 'girl next door' kind of way but Niki had something special. Her dark olive complexion and raven black locks gave her a Mediterranean guise and, even without makeup, she was incredibly attractive. She could have literally dated any one of the hordes of men who frequented the local bars, but she settled for Pete. The driving instructor with zero personality, average looks and a heavy dose of OCD.

Sometimes Sophie believed her attraction to Pete might be nothing more than a desire to stay in their friendship group. He was a good friend of Carl's and it was that friendship that had brought her into the lives of the other two girls. Whatever her reasons, Sophie still thought she was wasted on 'perfect Pete' as she sarcastically named him due to his obsession with order and 'things in rightful places'.

"I'm sorry Nik. You'll be late for work." It was not a genuine apology, it was a bid for sympathy, aimed at provoking unconditional support.

"I don't care, I'll ring in sick if I have to. What's wrong?"

Sophie knew if she played the humble card Niki would step up.

"What happened to you? You look dreadful."

Sophie sighed deeply as she was deciding how much she should divulge. It seemed strange to be trying to tell Niki again, but she needed help and this time she knew she should keep to the facts about her and John to herself and not complicate the situation with tales of a dual existence.

She started with the day Carl stood her up and her evening with John. There was little reaction from Niki, causing her to wonder if this was the same person she had already told the story to, but after a few moments Niki interjected.

"Well, I'm not surprised really the way you were talking last Friday. I had a feeling you might be about to do something rash."

Sophie smiled, registering the fact that Friday had taken place in both of these versions of her existence. It was the starting point. The moment everything started to change and somehow separate.

At least she was now in the place where John was hopefully a reality, and she could do nothing more than to tentatively make plans to move forward whilst desperately hoping she would not be catapulted back to the awful place where John was not.

Niki placed her hand on Sophie's to reinforce the support she was offering.

"So, what do I do now?"

"What do you want to do Soph?"

"I want to be with John and get out of my relationship with Carl, but I want to do it without hurting him."

"Well, that's realistic!" Niki said sarcastically causing Sophie to withdraw her hand, but Niki realised how her remark sounded and pulled back Sophie's hair to look her in the face. Their eyes met and nothing more needed to be said. They hugged and Sophie seemed to draw strength from it, strength compelling her to unburden herself further.

"I need to sort this out. I know that, but there is something else." Sophie was screaming at herself inside to shut up

"More? I don't think I can take any more" Niki laughed.

"Well not exactly more, but just something which is adding to my confusion," she had to stop talking. She had to shut up! "you see sometimes I keep thinking that I dream things that are real or the other way around and I don't know reality from dreams half the time." It was too late, the damage was done. Again.

"Now that is worrying."

"I know. Do you think I should see a doctor or something?"

"Definitely."

Now both versions of her friend thought she was a head case, and she was already loathing herself for being so weak and pathetic.

"I don't want to be labelled as a psychopath or something."

Niki took Sophie's hand in hers.

"You are not mad. I do think you need help though." It was the same look she had seen before. Her credibility was in question and her friend was treating her like a mental patient in need of incarceration. She sighed deeply knowing that all hope of an equal conversation had now evaporated in the heat of her despair.

"Sophie, you've had all this worry over a wedding you are not sure about, you've been worrying yourself sick and Carl has been working flat out for a deposit on a house that you don't even know you want."

"I know. I'm fine. I don't need a doctor."

"Yes, you do. I'm sure you can be prescribed something to help you until you sort out what you want. Once you've made your decision, I think you will stop having these nightmares, but you do need to see a doctor." Sophie could hear the panic in her friend's voice. She wanted to unburden herself of the responsibility for a mad woman and Sophie didn't blame her

"Ok. I will." Sophie was too exhausted to argue, "can I stay here for a while. I really don't want to go back to the flat just yet and I have no clothes for work. I'll take a taxi back to pick up some things later, if that's alright? You get off to work."

Niki was visibly horrified

"And leave you in this state? Not a chance. I'll run you back to the flat and come in with you in case he's still there. I could then drive you to your mum's if you want?" It was obvious Niki didn't want Pete to return to find Sophie in his house in this state but going to her mum's wasn't an option right now.

"I'd rather stay with you for a bit, if that's ok? I don't want to face mum and dad and all the questions over the wedding until I feel a bit stronger." She would never normally be this pushy, but she needed a safe space to think and it seemed like the only option.

"Yes. Of course." Niki smiled unconvincingly. She was now an unwelcome guest, but she didn't care as she laid her head on the breakfast bar and closed her aching eyes for a second.

"You look awful Sophie, why don't you take a shower and I'll find you some clean clothes to wear?"

"Thank you. I just feel so tired and worn out."

Upstairs in the shower, the warm water washed the salty tears from her face, soothing her tired body as it ran down her chest and stomach, but as the soapy water reached her grazed legs it stung and smarted as the sand was washed into the white shower tray below.

She stood for a while with the water pouring onto her closed eyes and tried to empty her head of all the terrible thoughts relentlessly looping. Fears that the only logical conclusion was that she was losing her mind.

She wrapped herself in the large warm towel from the rail and went into the spare room where a sweatshirt and a pair of joggers had been laid out for her. Probably in the hope that she would go to bed, and Pete might not need to be told of her presence at all. In the mirrored wardrobe she noticed her eyes were red with dark puffy circles below. Her face looked tense and drawn. She seemed to have aged a decade in one day and she felt that neither of the men who were competing for her, would find her even remotely attractive right now. She sat on the edge of the bed and leaned gently onto the pillow for comfort, hugging a pillow is something she had done since she was a small child but today it didn't offer the same solace.

Slowly she turned onto her back in the damp towel and listened to Niki making her call to work. Lying about a fake illness to comfort her friend or, more likely, to avoid leaving a mentally deranged person alone in her house.

She closed her eyes tightly to shut out the world for a few moments before she needed once again, to face the holy mess that had become her life.

"Sophie?" It was only a whisper, but she recognised Carl's voice immediately.

"Sophie?" He was gently shaking her, and she opened her eyes in panic that he had tracked her down. Niki had betrayed her!

"Where's Niki? How did you get in here?"

"Thank God. I thought you were ill or something." Carl's face was slowly coming into focus.

The panic of him finding her was swiftly overtaken by a different kind of panic when she saw a familiar painting over his shoulder. It was a painting in her own bedroom at the flat and yet here it was behind him as he was bent over her.

"Where are we?"

"You may well ask," he laughed "I have been trying to wake you for ages."

"I feel groggy." Was all she could say.

"I'm not surprised. The glass beside you smells of whisky! Did you start drinking after I came to bed?"

She tried to recall the whisky and where that fitted in to the events that had become so overlapped. She remembered drinking the whisky in the hope of provoking sleep so that she might dream of John again. John, who she had decided was an imaginary love, yet now she wasn't at all sure. She pulled the pillow around her face to mask her confusion until she could join the dots.

Through the padding of the pillow, she could hear her phone ringing and reached out to answer it.

"Sophie, its dad. Can you come to the hospital love? It's your mum. She's collapsed."

"What? Yes, yes, I'm on my way."

"What's wrong Sophie?" Carl knew immediately that something serious had happened.

"It's mum. She's in the hospital."

"I'll drive you." It was an order not a suggestion and she was grateful for his decisiveness.

He handed her some clothes, collected her bag, her phone and charger, put on his jacket and stood dutifully with his keys in hand while she fumbled with her buttons and tried to tie her laces with shaking hands.

It was still dark as they approached the car and Carl opened the door for her before taking the broken ice scraper from the side pocket and vigorously attacking the ice with all his might. He had asked for a heated one for Christmas, but she had failed to get him one. She hardly ever got him what he asked for, and as she watched him toil ferociously with the broken bit of plastic, she felt guilty. Guilty for all the presents that were more to her own liking than his, guilty for never really listening to his plans or ambitions, guilty for believing he wasn't enough for her and guilty for cheating on him to satisfy her selfish lust for romance.

As they drove along the dark country roads, she recalled the night before. The night Carl was aware of, while he contentedly made this silent drive. He was unaware that anything was wrong between them. The wedding planning was on track and so were they. He was happy with his lot and in the adversity of this uncertain drive, he was exactly where he ought to be, at the side of his future wife, supporting and comforting. Gushing with love and adoration for the person in his heart and in his bed. She envied him again.

Chapter 8

Half hour later she was running down a sterile corridor, frantically following signs and arrows, while Carl walked swiftly behind. The hospital stench of disinfectant with a sickly undertone of human body fluids filled her nose and mouth as she panted from exertion and anxiety.

As she turned the final corner, she saw a familiar figure fidgeting nervously at the end of the corridor. She had always regarded her father as a formidable figure but today he looked small and frail. He had shrunk into a helpless weak old man on the day she needed him to be strong and in control.

"What happened?"

His hair looked greyer and his face almost skeletal with worry.

"She was making toast and I heard a bang and found her on the kitchen floor."

"Did she regain consciousness?"

He shook his head.

"Have they told you anything?"

"Only that she is still unconscious."

"She's going to be fine." Sophie stated as though it were an indisputable fact. She needed to be strong for him, the way he had so many times for her. She put her arm around him as Carl moved to his other side, sandwiching him as though for protection.

"She probably just fainted dad." Sophie's tone was almost casual.

He nodded but there was much he wasn't sharing with his only daughter. He put an arm around her shoulders and whispered softly.

"I'm sorry love, she didn't want anyone to know."

"Know what?"

He held his head down for a while as though trying to avoid her question.

"Dad you are scaring me. Know what?"

His silence confirmed her worst fears.

"Is she ill?"

He raised his face to hers. The tears had formed in his eyes but were pooled and resting on his bottom lids. Gently he patted her shoulder as the words were starved of sound from his closed throat.

Sophie sobbed into her hands "Oh no! Please tell me she will be ok dad."

He had dreaded this moment, but he knew that sooner or later, he would have to watch his daughter endure this pain.

"She has a brain tumour, love."

Sophie clutched her chest as though she had been hit by a bullet.

"How long has she known? How bad is it? Can they treat it?" The questions all rolled into one

"She has only known for a few months and has started treatment but unless it shrinks soon, they can't operate."

"So, she will recover?"

He squeezed his daughter's hand "It's not likely love, but an operation will give her more time. We'll know more when the doctor comes back as she is having another scan right now."

Together they sat silently enduring the hours between each minute, until finally a doctor headed in their direction and herded them into a relative's room which Sophie knew was not a good sign.

The doctor's expression fuelled her fears further and Carl was already preparing himself to prop up his fiancé and father-in-law.

"We need to operate right away."

Sophie lost the use of her legs and wobbled towards Carl who already had her in his arms.

The doctor seemed to take pity on her and tried to negate the impact of the awful news he had delivered by adding a note of optimism.

"Once we remove the tumour, we can offer her more treatment."

"But I thought it was too big? Dad you said so?"

"We can't wait for it to shrink so we need to try to remove it before it damages her brain."

It was a tactical response. A clever way of dodging the words 'last resort' or 'desperate last attempt.'

"Can I see her?" Sophie stammered between sobs.

"Only for a minute as we need to move quickly. She's still unconscious though." The doctor warned

Sophie entered the room where her mother lay motionless. It was as though she were already dead. She sat beside the bed and picked up the lifeless hand now decorated with age spots, spots that she had never noticed before. Gently she kissed the unfamiliar hand and kept it close to her lips as she spoke. The words fell from her lips like a sinner longing to confess. How trivial 'men and weddings' had suddenly become when an hour ago they were the centre of her selfish world.

"Oh mum. I've been an idiot. I've been playing with fire, as you would say. I know what your advice would be so please come back so I can show you I do listen."

She kissed the freckled hand again and made a bargain with God, with fate, with whoever might judge her, as she vowed to give up this infatuation with the illusive John, if only her mum would recover. It was the only sacrifice she felt she had to bargain with, to show whoever might be listening how much she would give up for this. But even as her whispered bargain was being made, she was hoping God would not notice that somewhere deep in her soul, her virtual fingers were crossed to negate the lie.

She kissed her mum on the forehead and as she walked back down the corridor it occurred to her that her mother's illness had handed the perfect excuse to cancel her wedding. Of course, she couldn't use it and why would she want to, since she had just committed to staying with Carl? She had probably just been noticing the irony of it, of being provided with a reason at the very moment she no longer wanted one. Yes, that's all it was.

"Perhaps we should postpone our wedding?" She suggested, purely on the grounds that they would need to be sure mum would be fit to attend.

"Not likely!" her father said firmly "your wedding is what your mum is aiming for, she wants to see you on your wedding day more than anything. The longer you delay it the more likely she won't be able to make it."

Sophie's heart sank. It sank from self-loathing, from not realising a delay would steal her mum's dream but mostly because her wedding plans were still steaming ahead more powerfully than before.

She slumped back down beside Carl who immediately put his arm around her shoulder and gave her a squeeze in misguided appreciation and recognition of the sacrifice she has offered to make.

She didn't deserve these wonderful people. She didn't deserve the hug. She didn't deserve for her mum to live after her fake bargaining. But nor did she deserve to be teased by a love she couldn't have, or to be bouncing in and out of reality. She didn't deserve any of this!

She leaned on Carl, feeling suddenly that she should hate John (if he even existed at all) for making her abandon herself so completely. She pulled in closer to her reliable boyfriend, as though seeking protection from this obsession that had taken her over. She wanted to be good again, to be the kind faithful girl that gave her inner peace, she wanted to be wholesome again.

"Anyone want something from the vending machine?" It was a gesture of her resolve to be just that.

"Bar of chocolate would be nice." Carl smiled, he never refused chocolate.

Sophie smiled back and took out her purse. It felt good to be good, she acknowledged to herself. So why, at the very second she was out of sight, was she frantically checking her mobile phone for any message from John and searching through her contacts once again for his number?

She stopped in the corridor, she had tried to memorise it when she was with him and made a few attempts at remembering it, but it was no use. She did however remember his address in London and the name of his bank and found herself making plans to check them out, in person if necessary, just for the sake of her own sanity. This was the reason with which she justified her intention, but the undertone of self-hatred was already accusing her of a different motive entirely.

She took back drinks and sandwiches from the vending machine

"Chocolate?" Carl frowned as he checked over the fruits of her journey.

"Oh, I'm sorry. I'll go back."

"It's fine. I'll go, muddle head," he said affectionately as he kissed her head "this poor head has enough to think about without remembering my chocolate."

If only he knew! The chocolate was absent, but not because her mum was at death's door, the chocolate was absent because she had been desperately trying to contact her secret lover who caused her to behave like a selfish child.

The sandwiches she bought for Carl and dad remained unopened, no-one was hungry. She toyed with her own sandwich and found herself thinking of John again as she put together the two halves "Cut and shut" she smiled slightly and wished he were here to make her feel safe and warm.

The sound of purposeful footsteps jolted her from her shameful wishes.

"She is comfortable and won't wake up until morning at the earliest as she is heavily sedated after the operation, so I think you should all go home and come back tomorrow" The surgeon's suggestion was delivered in such a way that rendered it non-negotiable.

Darkness had started to fall, and they were grateful to be bullied into get some rest, but decided that they would all stay at Sophie's parents' house. An act of solidarity in a family crisis enabling them to comfort to each other. Calling at the flat for a few overnight things Carl and Sophie were soon on their way inland to her parents' country cottage.

Driving through the darkness in silence, Sophie was grateful to be excused from conversation while Carl searched desperately for something appropriate to say. He remained quiet and she remained content with her own thoughts. Her own thoughts which were taking her away from this world of heartache and unhappiness and into a world of dreams where John could hold her close and complete her.

They finally arrived and made their way up the overgrown pathway in the damp fog and into the warmth of the homely cottage. The smell hadn't changed. It was the smell that had greeted her every night after school. Freshly laundered linen, furniture wax and the sooty aroma of the cold deposits of the coal fire in the grate. The third kitchen floor tile was still chipped where she had dropped a full dish of casserole after trying to remove it with a towel instead of the oven glove, when she was thirteen. The cheap pot ornament of a lady in a long blue dress and bonnet still took centre stage on the mantel despite the fact that her parasol was chipped, and her right ankle had been stuck back together. She had bought it from her pocket money when she was six as a Christmas present for mum. Dad had taken her to the shop to choose something and she bought it although she thought the pink ballet dancer was much nicer and mum loved to watch the ballet. She pretended to prefer the blue one as it was cheaper and left her with enough money for sweets. Today she wished she had bought the ballerina.

Carl took her coat while she was still looking resentfully at the blue lady and guided her to a chair. He was armed with a bottle of whisky and poured a couple of large glasses for himself and his future father-in-law. Sophie was happy to be excluded from this masculine ritual and sought solitude in the bathroom from where she hoped to make a seamless transition into the bedroom and escape to the fantasy world which existed in the universe of her own mind.

She lay quietly on her childhood bed, surrounded by the familiar toys she had flippantly refused to take when her mum offered to pack them for her. Her favourite had been the hand-knitted rabbit. Partly because it was so delicately made with soft wool and tiny detail but mostly because it had been knitted in secret by her mum after she went to bed and given to her for no particular occasion. Somehow the totally unexpected gift gave it more value. She picked it out from the line up on the bed and put it up to her nose. It had a smell of its own and its arms and legs still dangled where the filling had fallen from the joints. It's tiny face with no chin, where it had been stretched to attach to the body still made her smile as she held it to her own, and remembered those happy carefree days. Such a contrast to the heavy burdens she was carrying now. She cradled the tiny rabbit in the pit of her arm and wished that tomorrow she would wake up for school with her lunch packed with Vimto, cheese and onion rolls and a Kitkat.

Restlessly she drifted back and forth between waking and sleeping hoping desperately to be reunited with John on whom she could lean at this awful time. She knew he would know exactly what to say, unlike Carl who now seemed more concerned for her dad than for her.

"Come on sleepy head," came a familiar female voice. The hairs on the back of her neck began to prickle as they raised from her skin. Niki put a cup of hot tea beside her and stroked her hair gently "let's go and get your stuff so I can get you settled in."

Sophie caught her breath and stared blankly. It had happened again! She was back at Niki's flat. This time, strangely, there was no feeling of terror.

Quickly she grabbed her phone and searched her contacts. There he was – she was back where she belonged and was excitedly sending John a text without a thought for anything other than finding him again.

"'Can you meet me at lunchtime? Carl knows. I have left him…… and my mother is really ill" she added clumsily.

He replied instantly

"So sorry. Yes of course – our place at one? Don't worry. I'm here always xxx"

She hugged the phone tightly and thought that if only he knew – if only he really was there always.

"Was that him?" Niki's voice was soft and warm.

"Yes," she nodded "what time is it?"

"Just after ten. You fell asleep. I've spoken to Kelly and she is faking a migraine and joining us"

Her phone beeped a second time and she picked it up quickly and then froze for a moment when she saw the sender – Mum!.

Hands shaking, she opened the message.

"Been trying to think of something to get Dad for his birthday, any ideas?"

She closed her eyes tightly. Her mum was fine – of course she was.

"Oh God, thank you!" She kissed the phone gently and then smiled widely

"Are you alright?" Niki asked witnessing this sudden passion for her phone

"I am now." She text back, "Perhaps take him somewhere? I love you so much"

"I think he might think I've lost the plot." Came the reply with a smiley face which Sophie had shown her how to make with symbols. Sophie made her own smiley face on reading it.

Her bargain with God was no longer needed. Her mum was fine.

Chapter 9

"Come on Sophie," Niki urged "you need a bit of a makeover if you are going out in public. You look a mess."

"Really, there's no need," Sophie protested "I can do all that at the flat when I can get to my clothes and my own makeup."

She thought for a moment, there was a chance Carl had not gone to work so she should probably do the best she could. She sighed audibly at the thought of a confrontation with Carl.

"Perhaps I could borrow a clean blouse and a bit of makeup after all. In case Carl is still there?" She smiled trying to hide the anticipation of her meeting with John at one o'clock and the dread that she may not get chance to clean herself up if she couldn't get into the flat alone.

"Make up? Just to go back to the flat for your stuff? I'm sure I can find you something to tide you over," Niki offered, "something you can at least go out on the street in. I mean, it's not like you have a hot date with your new Adonis is it?"

Sophie smiled to herself. If only Niki could see him. Adonis indeed!

She was right about one thing though. Sophie was giving far too much attention to sprucing herself up. She would be the first to say she shouldn't care. It wreaked of insecurity, yet she was rummaging through Niki's wardrobe for something bright and colourful, regardless of how expensive or new it looked. When she finally picked out an emerald green chiffon blouse, she held it up for Niki's approval totally ignoring the reaction that clearly showed her friend's dismay. The tag was clearly visible, it was obviously unworn, yet Sophie was not deterred and continued to hold it up until her friend nodded uncomfortably.

Borrowing makeup did not go smoothly either, as Niki's complexion was much darker so, having applied the base, she had to remove it and settle for mascara and lipstick. She hoped Carl had got himself out of her way as she would not be happy turning up like this. By the time they picked up Kelly from the salon, anger was building inside her as she suspected he might have taken to his bed like a lovesick puppy and already she was despising his unconfirmed weakness.

As they pulled up outside, Sophie noticed just how few residents were left in the block. The area had really gone downhill in the two years they had been there, and many were already boarded up. The landlord had been unable to find new tenants for many of the poorly maintained dwellings in the block. Carl had often joked that when they married and bought a place of their own, the owner would breathe a sigh of relief and demolish the lot.

"I need to go around the back and check if his car is there." Sophie called, as she got out of Niki's car.

"You look very controlled," Kelly snapped "almost happy!" she seemed disappointed that Sophie wasn't falling apart.

"It's amazing what love can do isn't it?" Niki's tone was also less than sympathetic, almost sarcastic, not realising that Sophie's determined strides were born of pent-up anger towards Carl. Anger at the possibility that he might try to stand between her and her makeup bag.

After a few moments Sophie beckoned from the front of the flat and the two girls made their way over and followed Sophie up the flight of stairs to the dwelling they had visited on many happier occasions.

While she set about packing her clothes and getting changed, Kelly and Niki sat in the living room exchanging whispers, whispers she could hear clearly through the flimsy stud wall.

"Should we say something?" Kelly whispered, "she's being a damn fool!"

"No. She wouldn't thank us for it. All we can do is to be here for her"

"She's far too happy about all this. I bet she's planning a bit of afternoon delight"

"Surely not" Niki laughed, "she's not that heartless."

"You think?" Kelly hissed sarcastically.

In the bedroom Sophie gritted her teeth and fought the temptation to respond, she was executing her plan and an altercation with her collaborators right now would be a disaster. First and foremost, she would make herself presentable and then she would deal with the task of disentangling herself from Carl. These were practical tasks and her emotions had been duly disengaged. She was doing him a favour in saving him from a miserable marriage. She was giving him the freedom to find his own true love the way she had found John. At no point did she allow herself to consider that he had already done so.

With the resolve, determination, and single mindedness of having a suffering animal destroyed, Sophie approached the task of destroying Carl's life with a clear conscience. All for his own good, no room for dilly dally.

It was in this practical, and somewhat ruthless frame of mind that she decided to write Carl a note. She reached into the drawer for a pad, quickly tearing off the latest 'for and against' list which she flicked into the bin. Then taking the pad and pen into the living room she sat on the sofa between her friends.

"Is this a 'dear John' letter?" Kelly asked sarcastically, emphasising the irony of the name

"I have no idea what I want to say to him."

Kelly unleashed her annoyance at Sophie's behaviour.

"How about... Thought I wanted you but seen something better so I'm off. Sorry for ruining your life?"

Niki shot her a reprimanding glare, but she shrugged unapologetically "What's the point in dressing it up? She knows he's in love with her but she's just a bit bored with it and thinks she deserves better. I'm sorry, I don't want to judge but I think this is a selfish ego-fuelled mistake."

Niki put her hand on Sophie's.

"Ignore her Sophie," she smiled, "Kelly wants an uncomplicated life and she wants everyone to be content and that's fine but if you are looking for something to take your breath away then that's fine too. We all have to make our own choices."

Kelly studied her nails for a moment defiantly and then sighed deeply

"I'm sure your new man is everything Carl is not," the comment was open to interpretation "and don't worry we will help him to get over you," this sounded more like a threat than reassurance.

"Well, you will meet him soon." She replied, failing to acknowledge the inference

Sophie picked her pen back up and decided the addressee was too obvious to include so she got straight to the point;

"Please don't think that I don't love you or that you have not been an incredibly special part of my life. I just need to take some chances and follow some rainbows, or I would live the rest of my life wondering if there is more out there for me. I may regret this, and if I do you can revel in my misery. I am so sorry for hurting you and I hope you find someone very special who will make you realise that I was nothing special.

Take care of yourself …Sophie X

The few tears that formed in her eyes were quickly reabsorbed before ever falling as she folded the paper and propped it on the table against a photograph of her and Carl kissing.

"Really?" Kelly shrilled.

Sophie looked back at the note resting on the couple's half-closed eyes and quickly picked it up and propped it against a vase instead.

"Satisfied?" she smiled.

"Bloody stunned." Kelly muttered as if intended only for Niki but intentionally a little louder

Sophie chose not to rise to the bait. "Come on let's get out of here," she said faking a sniff and wiping the imaginary tears across her face with her sleeve. "now see what a state I look again"

Kelly shook her head. The fake tears had no impact on her appearance. In fact, she looked positively radiant. Her face perfectly covered with a pigmented foundation giving her a radiant shine and her lashes curled back to frame her almond shaped brown eyes. The hint of blusher so discreet it could be mistaken for a healthy glow and pink lip gloss only a shade darker than her natural lips. She had pulled her hair through a loose band from which uncaptured strands fell randomly to frame her face. Kelly couldn't help but comment.

"You actually look great." Kelly sighed sulkily.

Sophie seemed genuinely shocked "I don't think so, look at you, you look perfect."

"Yes, look at me. A perfectly painted doll, a work of art. It's my job isn't it? but for once I wish I could look like that."

"Like what?"

"Just naturally, carelessly, almost accidentally sexy." Kelly couldn't resist voicing her professional opinion even though complimenting Sophie was a consequence.

Sophie smiled as a new confidence grew visibly and Kelly gave herself a virtual kick for causing it.

"Would you drop me at the White Heart and take my bags back to yours Niki?"

"Ah, you are meeting John?" Niki glanced at Kelly by way of apology.

"Yes. Do you mind?"

"Does it matter?" Kelly interjected but Niki cut her off.

"No of course not." Niki's tone was warm, but Sophie could sense that her friends' support was weakening as their sympathy was shifting towards Carl. It was difficult to suppress her excitement, but she made a mental note to try. After all, she needed Niki's hospitality until she could make plans.

As she sat in the back of Niki's car, among the bags in which she had stuffed most of her worldly possessions she was conscious of something much more disturbing than her lack of sentiment for Carl.

She had once again moved from reality to dream or from dream to reality and continued to live as though this were normal. How could she have come to accept this totally abnormal life?

She remembered once hearing that a person can learn to get used to anything in time and the abnormal becomes normal but surely not something like this. Her promise to see a doctor had been an empty one prompted by the niggling questions she was trying to ignore. She was not going to risk anything that might somehow spoil this moment.

She smiled as she jumped out of the car realising that no amount of unanswered questions was capable of calming the little butterflies that were dancing mercilessly in her stomach.

Chapter 10

The sight of his car already parked, whipped the butterflies into a frenzy and her hands were shaking as she reached for the door handle.

Unlike the trendy pub she frequented with her friends, the White Heart (their pub as she named it) was traditional, a little dark with a log fire and quaint soft furnishings. She glanced around, noticing a few couples deep in conversation over lunch and then a pair of feet sticking out from behind a dividing wall that she knew instinctively, were his. How could someone's lower legs be recognisable she thought, yet they were his and she knew it.

She peeped around the corner "Hi."

"Hi yourself." He winked.

She winked back and he laughed out loud.

"What?" she asked disdainfully.

"You can't wink?"

"Maybe I never had anyone I wanted to practise it on?"

He stood up and pulled her towards him by the hand.

"Well thank God for that." He kissed her cheek.

She noticed he had already got her a glass of wine, so she slid in behind the table and he sat back down beside her.

"So, what's happened? and what's wrong with your mum?"

She had forgotten she had told him about her mother and needed to back pedal quickly.

"Oh. It was a false alarm. She's ok now."

He frowned “It sounded serious?”

“I thought it was, but it wasn’t.”

He shrugged as though confirming that although he thought there was more to it, he was prepared to let it go.

She noted the suspicion on his face, but short of telling him her mother was ill in a different existence, she had to be satisfied with his expression of mistrust.

Luckily, he didn’t press her and changed the subject.

“So, what about you and Carl?”

“I’ve left him,” she said triumphantly “are you ok with that?”

He took her hand in his “I’m delighted”

“Really?”

“Really”

“It’s all moving so fast though. I mean, we hardly know each other really?”

“Well, I think we might be about to now you’re a free woman.” He winked.

She smiled and kissed him gently, but he returned it more passionately until she pulled away. She felt suddenly irritated that he had made a joke at Carl’s expense.

“We’re in public Casanova!” She didn’t want to reprimand him, but she needed a moment. She just wished he had shown a little respect for Carl and some appreciation of what she had done to free herself for him.

“So, let’s fix that.” He winked again, insinuating that they find a private place for some intimacy.

Her heart sank for a moment at his insensitivity, but it was only a fleeting moment. Quickly she dismissed his behaviour as nothing more than careless excitement and consequently he was vindicated. She did, however, refuse to be drawn into the childlike mischievousness by failing to acknowledge his comment.

"So, what do we do now?" She said in a serious tone, making sure to effectively dampen his misplaced playfulness.

"This afternoon or long term?" He seemed to have got the message.

"Longer term." She clarified almost sternly, hoping he wouldn't disappoint her again.

"Well, I'm going back to London at the weekend but if you can get time off, why don't you come stay with me for a while? It'll give us chance to decide how to sort things out."

He had redeemed himself. It was exactly what she hoped he would say, and although she knew there were some difficult conversations ahead, she couldn't think of anywhere she would rather be than in the safety of his arms away from this mess.

"You really want me to come with you?"

"I said it didn't I? Maybe you will find me intolerable and you could slip back into your old life before anyone notices."

She knew he was joking but she didn't like the thought that he was even suggesting failure.

"That won't happen." She was looking directly into his eyes and they were telling her everything she wanted to know. If this was a mistake, then it was worth making because the emptiness without him was the only thing she had found intolerable since the moment he had handed her the contents of her handbag.

"I'll ring work later and ask for some leave days next week. I'll also need to speak to mum and dad about the whole wedding thing, so that they can start making some calls. I'm really not looking forward to that conversation."

As she spoke these words, she silently thanked God again that her mum was in good health. Of course, she felt guilty at putting them through the stress of a cancelled wedding, but it was a small inconvenience in comparison to the hell they were facing less than a day before. If that day had taken place at all.

For the first time since she had met John, they had a date without making love. There were too many problems to solve, too many issues to deal with, and she was hoping she was not the only one who was unable to crave physical pleasure right now. Yet somewhere deep inside, there was still a small part of her longing for his touch, and she knew it wouldn't have taken much to ignite that flame, despite the inappropriateness of it.

The entire afternoon passed quickly, and once they started to focus on practical plans, every hurdle felt less daunting. Her earlier resolve to maintain a respectful air of remorse for Carl started to crumble, as she failed time and again to contain her excitement.

This man had plans, huge plans, and based on what he'd achieved so far, she knew his ambition was no pipe dream. He was more than the man she loved, he was a man who was going places and he was taking her with him. She had hit the jackpot and suddenly the turmoil and emotion of the present started to fade to monochrome, against the vibrant colours of the future he was painting.

She munched happily on half a meat pie and half a slice of gammon without noticing that, as they made plans, she joined in without once considering Carl. She was displaying the same kind of childish selfishness that had disgusted her only a few hours before. Carl's broken heart had no place in hers, because hers was already full of joy. Dreams of a large house in the suburbs and eventually, a family of their own, had filled it to bursting point.

This wonderful man had laid out the yellow brick road before her eyes in a single afternoon, and she was going to march down it right into Emerald city. The possibility that it may all turn out to be as false as the story, was dismissed as recklessly as her false promise to God. She was making plans with the man she loved, and quite bluntly nothing else mattered, and anyone who didn't like it could go to hell.

She left John in the car park after a tender kiss and promised to contact him the next day to make arrangements to travel back to London with him at the weekend, but the need to keep him in her sight until then was immense. She was so afraid of falling asleep again and waking up in a world where he didn't even exist. Where Carl was her future. She wanted to tell John to take her to London right now, but she knew it would sound desperate and irrational. Disguising insanity is a very delicate business.

Back at Niki's, she hadn't noticed the time and was quite surprised when it was Pete who opened the door looking extremely uncomfortable. She wondered if Carl had spoken to him and she was now, not so welcome here.

Pete smiled weakly and returned to loading the dishwasher, leaving Sophie to make her own way in, and making no attempt at a conversation. She was grateful when Niki appeared from the bathroom wrapped in a towel.

"We have saved you some pasta if you're hungry Soph?"

"No thanks, I really have lost my appetite," she lied "I'll just watch some TV if that's alright? and tomorrow I'll get out of your hair."

"There is no need honestly."

She noticed the glance between them.

There was nothing honest about the comment.

She wished she had stayed with John. It hadn't seemed like an option but already she could feel that her friends were taking sides. She went up to the guest room and turned on the TV as a distraction. There was the usual selection of soaps, an episode of Cracker and a wildlife documentary. She tried to make sense of the detective story, but her concentration didn't seem to last more than a few minutes until she had seen so little of it, she no longer knew what it was about.

Niki popped in a couple of times to check that she was alright but seemed reluctant to stay for long and was obviously feeling torn between her and Pete. Her biggest concern right now was staying awake until morning as she was terrified of waking up God knows where with God knows who.

She tried to find something else to watch to keep her awake but was fairly confident that it didn't matter too much as it was unlikely that she would fall asleep with her head so full of questions and problems to solve.

There were moments when temporarily, she was distracted by a compelling murder mystery, finding herself pulled into the plot. But the moment her eyes left the screen, her heart was racing, followed by a tightness in her chest as reality replaced fiction and she was reminded of the vast step she had taken. It was a bitter-sweet emotion. Excitement and dread in equal parts. If only she had met John before Carl, if only Carl didn't love her so much, if only her friends didn't love Carl so much, if only, if only but here she was torn between loving and being loved and someone had to get hurt. Today it felt like everyone was getting hurt including her.

Still staring at the screen and trying to remember if the man with the hairy chest was married to the woman he was in bed with, she started to feel angry that her moment was being spoiled. This was the time of her life that should have been full of joy. She was finally in love and making plans for a future, but because of the timing of it, no-one was rejoicing with her and it all felt so tainted and awful.

Staying awake started to become a bit more difficult. Although her head was full of the issues she would face in the next few days, she was also emotionally exhausted. She propped herself into a sitting position, in order to hold off any temptation to rest her head, but her eyelids repeatedly slid down over her eyes.

She started to sing songs in a whispered voice and pinched the skin on her arm every time the lyrics started to drone away. She had to stay awake. She picked up the glass of water from the bedside table and flicked it onto her face at regular intervals to fend off the slumber that was pacing expectantly at the gate of her consciousness.

A couple of times her body twitched and jumped, and she checked frantically that she was still in Niki's bedroom and that John's number was still on her phone. All was well. Maybe at last this nightmare was over and the universe had resettled into its natural order. Perhaps the storm had passed and now she could relax in the quiet aftermath. A little more comforted she allowed herself to close her eyes and doze for a moment or two. She awoke with a start and checked the room. All was still well. She smiled contentedly.

She was comforted by the familiar face of a teddy bear. She knew him well; she had kissed him goodnight a million times and she pulled him to her affectionately. An affection that lasted several moments until the gravity of this reunion caused the blood to drain from her face and the fist of dread to close once again around her heart. This was 'little Ted' and little Ted resided at her childhood home. She thrust him away for the traitor that he was and sat up among the sickening familiar furnishings of her old bedroom.

"No! No! No!" She was screaming out loud holding her head as though about to rip it off in anger. She could smell the stench of whiskey and opened her eyes to see Carl's face only inches from hers as his arms engulfed her until he thrust himself upright in fright.

"What is it? What's happened?"

Sophie couldn't speak. Even if she could, there was nothing she could say to him. Instead, she put her head in her hands and started to cry.

"It's ok baby. She's in the best place and she's a fighter." He whispered.

"I need a doctor!"

Carl pulled back and cupped her face in his hands staring her right in the eyes.

"You are going to be fine."

"No, I'm not – I'm not fine. I need a doctor, please take me to a doctor!"

"Why do you need a doctor? Is it your head?" He asked as she continued to hold it in her hands

"No. It's not my head. I think I am losing my mind!" It was a confession she had desperately wanted to supress.

"Ok" He comforted "I'm not surprised you feel anxious. I'll take you in the morning"

"I need to go now Carl. I'm frightened." Suddenly she was relying on Carl again and felt like she was using everyone, but Carl was here, and John wasn't, and she needed something, someone and she needed them now.

She held onto Carl who hugged, patted and cajoled her into waiting until morning as he gently encouraged her to get under the covers and sleep. This could be sleep that would return her to John, but she was too afraid and shaken to even think of it. She needed to get well, and which world that meant living in, had become less important than this utter terror.

"I need to talk to dad."

"Leave him Soph, he's asleep."

"Did he say anything about mum's symptoms?"

"A bit, why?"

"Did she have dreams?"

"He said she got confused from time to time and sometimes she hallucinated."

"Oh my God!"

"What is it?"

Sophie couldn't speak for a moment. She knew. There was no doubt. She felt her head with her hands as though checking it for something.

"I think I have the same thing. It can be hereditary can't it?"

"I have no idea Sophie but you're imagining this. You've had a shock and believe me, there's nothing wrong with you. But if you want me to take you to the doctor tomorrow, so you're not worrying all weekend I will. He'll probably give you something to help you to cope."

"Thank you." She held onto him in a way she hadn't for a long time. Taking his hand firmly in hers she curled up in the nook his body provided. It felt like a warm safe cave and as she gently closed her eyes, she kept his loyal hand softly in hers.

Chapter 11

She awoke and looked around sleepily. The floral print curtains, the multi-coloured bedspread and Carl's hand still loosely in hers. After a night's sleep she felt stronger and refreshed. Carl's hand fell away as she slid from under his arm and padded over towards the bathroom.

She had slept and actually stayed in the same place. It was a double-edged sword. She had stabilized but she had done so in the world she was hoping was not her reality. She scrubbed and scrubbed as though trying to prove she was real and then let the water sooth her sore skin before wrapping a towel around her once again and opening her bag to pick out something to wear.

She couldn't be bothered to put together an outfit, or to think of her appearance at all and simply pulled out a pair of jeans and a sweater. The jeans which used to be tight around her hips felt loose and ill fitting. She pulled out the waistband and noted the several inches of surplus denim, she had not been eating well and that could be the cause, but in her mind, it was further confirmation that she was medically ill.

In the car, Carl tried to keep hold of her hand, recapturing it quickly every time he needed to change gear. Neither of them spoke and Sophie was trying to decide just how much she should tell the doctor. As the car pulled up outside the surgery, she decided she must tell him everything.

She left Carl in the waiting room and took a deep breath before starting to tell him the symptoms of her self- diagnosed brain tumour. He listened intently without interruption, his grey emotionless eyes fixed loyally in her direction and only the slight raising of his greying eyebrows and the occasional deepening of his crow's feet testified to the fact that he was paying attention to every word.

Doctor Walker had treated her for measles and tonsillitis and had sat on her bed at home a hundred times during her childhood, bringing the scent of the cold wet outdoors into her warm room on his long wool coat. She trusted him completely.

She told her story meticulously without worrying about how ludicrous it all sounded because she felt that the crazier she seemed, the more likely he was to offer help. It was a relief not to hold anything back. This was no time to harbour secrets. Even if he committed her, she would at least get the right medication to return her to some sort of stable existence.

Her story ended with her visit to the doctor and at this point he toyed with his pen silently before speaking.

"Do you think that today is reality or a dream?"

"I have no idea."

He smiled at her response which he thought was encouragingly humorous for someone so troubled.

"Can you see colours? Smell things? Taste things?"

"Yes why?"

"Well usually, in dreams, these things are not possible as it's your memory and imagination working, not your senses"

She appeared to be studying him, or at least the validity of what he had just said when he continued.

"In this world where this John exists, I bet you can't remember the taste of the sandwiches?"

"Not specifically but I think I must have."

"Did you smell his aftershave? The hot chocolate? What colour was his shirt?"

She thought for a moment. She hadn't noticed the smell of any aftershave and couldn't remember smelling the hot chocolate but it's not exactly something one commits to memory. She frowned for several moments as she struggled to validate his theory, then she remembered

"Orange! His tee shirt was orange!"

"Do you remember seeing that or was it a thought you had?"

She pondered for a moment. It had amused her that he wore something so outrageous.

"I think it was a thought."

The doctor smiled smugly.

"Do you see now that these dreams you are having are purely that? You are inventing your own fantasies. That's exactly what dreams are. They come from our own minds, nowhere else."

She tried desperately to think of something that would contradict what he was saying but couldn't.

"So why are they so real, why do they keep following on from one another and why are they lasting so long?"

"That's what we need to find out, but I can assure you that these are not symptoms of a brain tumour. This is most likely a sleep disorder and the first thing we need to do is to allow you to sleep more deeply so that your brain is not so active. I'm prescribing something to help you to do this and I want you to come back in a week to see how you are getting along."

She took the prescription and left the surgery, took Carl's hand and walked back to the car feeling several emotions she couldn't share and didn't want to. Carl dropped her off at the hospital on his way to work and she was grateful to be alone with her thoughts for a while.

Her mum was awake and in amazingly good spirits. She sat for over an hour talking to her and dad and although her words were slow and her breaths were shallow, she vowed that she was going to get well again and wanted to talk about the wedding. Sophie wanted to make sure she had a goal and enthusiastically planned the detail of place settings and little favour parcels. This was exactly what a mother and daughter should be doing and despite her own issues, she found herself warmed by it.

On the way home in dad's car, she felt more positive and more in control than she had for quite some time. She picked up her prescription on the way and smiled to herself "Sleep disorder!" She thought she had met the love of her life and he was nothing more than a sleep disorder. Love? She didn't believe in it anymore, not in the all- consuming romantic sense anyway, she believed in a quieter love, a more rational love, a love that didn't destroy everything in its selfish path.

Emerald City and had been exposed. The cruelty born of lust and passion, the destruction born of desire and self-indulgence, the misery dealt in the name of love.

As night fell and Carl returned home, she sat contentedly at the dining table planning mum's return home and how, as a team, they would help her through the battle ahead. She was determined not to let anyone down. She had been given a glimpse of how it felt to be the wanton woman, the heartbreaker and the shameful daughter and she didn't like it. Not one bit.

After supper she took her pills and went to bed leaving Carl and her dad to watch a late thriller on TV. She stopped at the door and turned back to look at the two men in her life. Her love for her dad was unquestionable and this new feeling of warmth towards Carl was comforting and secure. She had a good man. She had done well.

Lying alone in bed she reassured herself that everything would be fine. Her life was good. It was complete and she was surrounded by love. There was a small void where her dream had lived. Where John had lived. His gentle touch, his cheeky smile, the way he seemed to know her so well, but of course he did, because she had invented him so how could he not? She went over every moment with him checking each one for validity that he was fictional. Everything stacked up.

She thought his eyes were brown but couldn't really remember seeing them, she couldn't remember the colour of his suits or even his car. The more she accepted that he was someone of her own invention the more easily she started to fill in the void he had left, but as the void began to close the feeling of sorrow grew.

She told herself over and over that there was no John, dismissing every one of her memories of him but there was one thing she could not dismiss with logic and that was this very strong feeling of his presence, the essence of his being, and it felt just as powerful now as it ever had. In her heart she felt him, and he lived, and she thought it impossible that she could create the spirit and essence of someone who didn't exist. She could still feel him.... everywhere.

Later that night she stirred slightly as she felt Carl snuggle up behind her, his familiar shape and smell, and was grateful for the warmth of him. Tomorrow was Friday and she decided to take the afternoon off to visit mum and then do something special with Carl in the evening.

The daylight shone through the pale curtains completely lighting the room, more rudely than she remembered it, on those sleepy school mornings before her mum had thrown them open to shock her eyes into accepting that morning had arrived.

She reached behind her to a cold empty space where Carl had been the night before and could hear whispered exchanges of conversation from the next room. She lifted her head from the pillow to listen more closely.

One of the voices sounded like Niki's and the other was male but less familiar. It was definitely not Carl or her dad and out of the corner of her eye she could see that her prom photo had been replaced by a print of a sunflower. This was Niki's flat, and this would be Thursday.

She no longer had the energy to fight or to resist the inevitable and merely pulled the duvet over her head and took a deep breath before entering another day in which her mum would be well, her father happy, her lover waiting, her friends hostile and her boyfriend heartbroken.

For a moment she allowed herself to reflect on the fact that it was indeed Thursday. Had it really been less than a week since she had met her friends for after work drinks? She remembered taking a moment to commit it to memory before entering the bar and, in comparison to now, her life had been a breeze.

She rang work and asked for a week's holiday at short notice due to personal reasons. At first Paul was unreceptive, trying to exert his authority, reluctant to set a precedent but when she argued that it was hardly the busy season and reminded him of the favour she had gained with those far above his paygrade, his tone changed. He was caught off guard by the dogged determination in her voice and backed down. She smiled at the speed at which he ended the call and wished she had been this confrontational more often. She was still smiling when she called John.

"Hi."

"Hi. How's it going?"

"Is there any chance we could leave today?"

"Well, I wasn't planning to go home until the weekend, what's the rush?"

"I'm at Niki's but things are not so welcoming here and I don't want to talk to mum and dad yet so I could really do with getting out of this place"

"Do you want me to book you a hotel for a couple of nights?" It was not the response she was hoping for.

"No, it's fine. I really don't want to be alone so I'm probably better staying where I am." She didn't try to conceal the emotion in her voice, hoping he would realise a hotel alone was not what she had been hoping for.

"Hey what's wrong? Are you crying?"

"No." She lied without even trying to stop her voice breaking.

"If mi lady is in need of rescue, she should keep an eye on the castle gate," he joked, "I'll pack my things and pick you up this afternoon."

"Thank you" she said gratefully, inwardly cursing that he had been so slow on the uptake. As she slammed and stuffed her belongings into bags, still annoyed at having to push him into collecting her, she reminded herself that he was a man, and men often need pushing. After all, he was on his way now and if she didn't calm down, he might just dump her off again. Slowly she allowed the doubt to melt away and within a few minutes she was already longing to feel his arms around her again.

She didn't go downstairs but watched out of the window until she saw Pete leave for work. Downstairs Niki was almost ready for leaving too. She was dressed in a smart trouser suit and her hair was tied neatly at the nape of her neck. She would have worn something more casual if this were Friday, something also suitable for their after-work drinks. Further confirmation that this was Thursday, although she assumed that the Friday ritual would now be cancelled – probably forever.

She fumbled through the three bags she had managed to pack. Everything was crumpled and some of the clothes hadn't even been washed. One bag was full of party dresses and another was crammed with shorts and tee shirts. What had she been thinking? She had brought hardly anything of immediate value.

As she folded a pair of pink shorts she wondered if she would still be with John in the summer months and be wearing any of these in her new home. She peered into the final bag and was relieved to find it stuffed with winter clothes, she pulled out a pair of leggings and an oversize sweatshirt which she laid on the bed and then tried to smooth out the creases with the warmth of her hand. It had no impression at all on the road-mapped fabric, so she pulled it over her head, pulled on the leggings and tied her hair up in a bun. She needed to check with Niki if it was alright to stay in the flat for the morning, so she reluctantly made her way to the kitchen.

"I'm sorry I dragged you into all this Niki."

"It's fine Soph," Niki replied without turning round from the toast she was clearly monitoring, "it's just difficult with Pete being so close to Carl."

Sophie wished she could see her face to judge the mood.

"I know. Has he heard from Carl?"

"Yes."

"How is he?"

"How do you think?" It wasn't a question and Sophie felt the judgemental tone like a slap in the face.

"I'm sorry – I'll leave."

Niki turned to face her at last. She hoped her friend was about to tell her there was no need and would stop her as she put her hand back on the bedroom door to collect her things right away. Niki said nothing as Sophie slid through the door and returned wearing a coat and laden with bags.

"Sophie?"

Sophie stopped with her hand on the door handle. Niki pulled her back gently by the shoulder and hugged her tightly.

"Take care of yourself."

Sophie's heart sank.

"You too." Sophie opened the door and then added "Take care of Carl too."

Niki nodded, the tears spoiling her freshly applied foundation.

Sophie walked to the café at the end of the street where she ordered a cooked breakfast which she poked periodically over the next two hours before the assistant eventually concluded that it was now congealed to the point of inedibility. The tea had been poured and sipped at prolonged intervals until the pot was empty so she ordered another pot and a doughnut in the hope it would last her until John's arrival.

Her stomach was churning, and the doughnut was consequently smuggled into her bag in bite size pieces as she drained another pot of tepid tea. Her white stallion arrived eventually in the form of the familiar red sports car which she had spotted long before he blew the horn to get her attention.

As she picked up her bags, she heaved a sigh of relief. By the time she got outside he was already standing on the pavement. His brandless jeans lost in the recess of his overhanging stomach hardly met the bottom of his projecting polo shirt. He was no Knight in armour, but he was saving her just the same. Saving her from so many things, herself included.

He got out of the car and she hugged him close, he squeezed her hand reassuringly as he unburdened her from her bags and from so much more. He threw them into the boot and smiled gently.

"I love you." She couldn't stop herself from saying it. She needed to say it. She needed to affirm it to justify the mess she was making.

"I love you too and we are going to be fine."

"I know." she said, as she hugged his neck and she knew, beyond doubt, that they would be.

"I've booked a hotel to break up the journey, its bit off route but I think you will like it."

"That sounds nice." she said quietly, unable to mirror his enthusiasm.

"Yes, I want to show you my favourite mountain. Let's start this as we mean to go on – good times ahead." His cheeky smile cracked the shell of her despair and she allowed herself to believe that all the grief would be worth it.

"How did this happen?" Sophie was not directing the question directly at John but more at the universe in general, "I mean, I've never been an impulsive person. I hardly know you. Do you really think this is love?"

"No. I'm just in it for the sex."

Sophie frowned for a moment and then laughed out loud at his sparkling eyes which were the only feature on his entire face that were grinning.

"I'm being serious. I don't know anything about you and yet I feel like you are.........."

"Home?"

"Yes, exactly. Is that how you feel?"

"Yup. I knew immediately. I recognised you instantly."

"Recognised me?"

"Yes. My wife."

Sophie felt tears of emotion rising at the back of her nose into her blurring eyes, emotion from her mother's illness, from Carl's tearstained face, from the days John deserted her, from the wrath of her friends. She was carrying the troubles from two lives simultaneously and opening her eyes widely could not prevent the tears from spilling onto her cheeks.

"Hey. We're ok," he smiled squeezing her knee affectionately, "if you want to know more, ask me a question. What do you need to know?" He was trying to lighten the mood

"Everything. Anything. Previous girlfriends, wives?"

"No wives, three serious girlfriends."

"What happened to them?"

"Nothing dramatic, just faded away I guess."

"Faded?"

"Yes. Started off slowly, all reached a level of habit, all shrivelled away quietly like cut flowers."

"The same may happen to us. What makes you think it won't?"

"Somehow I don't think so. We might break each other's hearts; totally destroy each other, but fade out? Never! We are not flowers and if we go out it'll be in a blaze of glory." He shuddered physically.

Gently she took his hand. "I won't break your heart"

"You don't know that"

"I do. It's my promise and I never break a promise. I would rather die"

"Die?"

"Yes. Wouldn't you rather die than betray me?"

"Of course I would." He joked, but she didn't laugh with him.

He frowned as he squeezed her hand in consolation, but there was something a little dismissive about it.

Chapter 12

The long drive from the village on the east coast to the Peak District had an air of holiday spirit about it as they switched radio channels, sang and tried to eat crisps and chocolate bars without messing up his immaculate car. She smiled and he scowled every time a morsel of food fell from her hand as she tried to feed both of them.

"How can anyone be so clumsy?" he said with a false smile as he watched another salt covered piece of crisp drop onto his shiny black carpet.

"I'll put them away." She smiled back, an equally false smile.

She stuffed everything back into the carrier bag and placed them on the back seat.

"You sulking now?"

"Nope," she lied "well a bit, maybe."

"You're bloody sulking."

"And you're a bloody kill joy!"

He stopped the car and looked at her for a moment then he pulled the crisps from the bag, took a handful and threw them in her face.

Her sulky face cracked into spontaneous laughter as she tried to remove the crisps from her hair and face.

"I love you." She smiled, kissing him with salty lips

"You better had," he replied "look at the state of my car!"

He pulled back onto the road as she tried to clear up the mess. A potential tiff had been avoided but his obsession with cleanliness had been duly noted. She would try not to annoy him in future.

The light was starting to fade as they winded their way along the last country lane. As they emerged from the trees on the final bend, the formidable, eerie shape of Mam Torr rose before them.

"She's quite something isn't she?" He said softly as he stopped the car to take in the view of his favourite place.

"Wow!" Sophie concurred, "it's magnificent"

They pulled into the hotel car park at the foot of the mountain and checked in. Their room was enormous with fresh white linen sheets and a spectacular view of the mountain which was now partly engulfed in freezing fog.

"Come on let's eat," he said tugging her towards the door, "I'm starving."

"Well, you should have eaten the crisps." She teased, wondering if she should maybe not have reminded him about the state of his car.

They sat at a table for two beside the window as he handed her a menu.

"What do you fancy?"

Sophie studied the menu for a few minutes and then grinned "Half and half?"

"You bet," he laughed, "smothered chicken and fillet steak?"

"Perfect." She took his hand and caught sight again of the magnificent imposing outline of the mountain against the dusky sky. White with snow and glistening in the moonlight.

"Let's go up there!" She said excitedly.

"Its winter and it's nearly dark!"

"If this is your favourite place, I want to go up there with you."

"We can go up there in the summer maybe." He consoled.

He didn't understand Sophie's need to grasp the moment while it was still within her grasp. She wasn't going to be fobbed off. She wanted to do this and to leave evidence that all of this was real.

"Didn't take you for a wuss." She teased hoping to goad him into taking up the challenge

"Wuss? I'll show you wuss!" he started to get up to start the accent there and then but then sat back down "maybe after we've eaten, there's a grumbling going on." He patted his stomach.

As they ate, Sophie was already starting to fear the night. If only she could find a way to stick a flag in the ground and claim this life. To hold it firmly in place.

She wasn't very hungry and after picking at the main course she settled for coffee while he devoured a large slice of chocolate fudge cake with cream. Her stomach was tightening as the dread of night crept into her. She watched him demolish his desert and smiled. She needed something, anything to try to anchor herself to this life and as she pondered, she toyed with the pepper pot. Perhaps she could write a note to herself and bury it somewhere? Preferably somewhere no-one could interfere with it.

He must have noticed the idea brighten her expression.

"What you planning in that head of yours?"

"Let's go up there and bury a time capsule. We can write a note and bury it in this." She held up the pot

"You're mad," he said, wiping the cream from his chin with a linen napkin, "and that's stealing by the way."

She tilted her head to one side pleadingly "We could come back here on our tenth anniversary and dig it up."

"You are actually serious?"

She picked up the menu "You got a pen?"

He took a pen from his pocket and handed it to her, shaking his head submissively.

"What do you want to record?" She smiled.

"I don't know. Date and time, I guess. Our names?"

She huffed "That's boring. I'm going to write that we are eloping."

"Eloping?" he echoed.

She blushed. She had gone too far and spoiled the moment. She kept her head down and tried to endure the silence, not knowing how to undo the damage. She pretended to be oblivious and started to write their names and the date.

"Eloping eh?" he said thoughtfully.

"I didn't exactly mean…."

He put his finger on her lips to silence her.

"Eloping it is then."

She scribbled onto the menu and then threw her arms around him. It wasn't exactly a proposal, but it was a huge hint and she loved it. Secretly she was already imagining telling the story to their future children. The beautiful children they would have if she managed to stay awake or to find some way of proving to herself that this was real. Something to give her the confidence to find her way back. She picked up the pepper pot.

"You better add something else," he grinned "say that if it's still here after ten years then we didn't make it."

Her heart missed a beat. Why would he say that? Was that something that came from her? Had she put those words into his mouth?

She looked at his grinning face. He had no idea of the importance of what he had said. She relaxed a little and continued writing in the blank spaces between the deserts and the wine list.

"Let's just go to bed instead. It's not a great idea to be going up there in this weather. We can go and get our money's worth out of that huge bed and do this thing in the morning."

She ignored his indifference. She didn't really care if he bought into this or not for, she had her own agenda in wanting to plant some physical evidence before nightfall. Before fatigue got the better of her and caused her eyelids to give up the fight. Before being transported quietly in her slumber back to that place where John would be nothing more than a memory. A ghost who would continue his haunting of her, from the place she couldn't reach.

It was illogical that it might manage to transfer itself to her other life when nothing else had, but somehow digging it deep into the side of a mountain where no-one could touch it or see it, seemed like a formidable anchor.

"Give me your finger?" she said as she took a safety pin from her bag.

"You gotta' be kidding me!" he snapped irritably, "blood brothers? What are you? Twelve?"

"Stop being such a grouch," she retorted playfully, "what use is a capsule without a bit of each of us?"

As she pricked his finger and wiped it onto the menu, she was starting to regret pushing him into something so juvenile, but she believed it might help her, one way or the other, in the near future so she folded and rolled up the bloodstained page of the menu and rammed it into the pepper pot before replacing the stopper. She picked up a spoon from the table and slipped both into her bag, smiled and nodded toward the door.

He gave a giant huff and rested his chin on his hand for a moment. She was standing above him, wating as he looked up at her through his heavy fringe.

"Well?" she asked.

He shook his head in disbelief that he was about to agree to this.

"I'll come but I'm not digging any bloody holes and if you get stopped for stealing that pepper pot as we leave the table you're on your own." His words seemed harsh but the raising of his eyebrows negated any sense of reprisal.

They returned to their room and put on warmer clothes before making their way to the foot of the mountain where man-made flagstones wove a path from ground level up to the summit.

Sophie was on a mission and set off with purposeful strides on the icy track, slipping repeatedly and grabbing John to recover her balance.

"I've seen enough." He laughed and left the path for the grassy track leaving her to fend for herself.

"Some gentleman you are!" She shouted into the wind, scrambling back onto her feet and throwing a playful punch in his direction.

They climbed the path, pressing down with their hands on their knees with each step as the gradient steepened. It was harder than Sophie had imagined and twice she stopped for breath, looked back at John who was too breathless to acknowledge her, and pressed on. Finally, they took the last few steps onto the snow- covered summit.

Aching legs and bruised lungs were forgotten as they stood together looking down through the patchy fog onto the world below. It was a magnificent sight and as John reached for her hand to reassure her that all was forgiven, she recognised the moment. This was the moment Carl had experienced. It was the moment she had spoiled by dropping her hand from is. She looked down at her hand firmly in John's. No one was loosening their grip this time, both hands were holding tight, this was love.

As the temperature dropped and the thick fog gusted up the slope beneath them, swallowing the base of the mountain they turned back onto the narrow path. Sophie started to look for a memorable spot to bury the pot, but the gravel path was flanked by the tough established grass of the mountain side.

"There's no way you are going to dig any of this up with a spoon," he snapped as though his irritation with her childishness had suddenly returned, "come on let's get back down while we can still see the way."

"Just give me one minute."

She stood by the manmade stone pile monument and took 6 large strides in the opposite direction to the path which took her to the border between grass and heather. She stopped and looked down at a large clump of mountain grass. At first, she tried to pull it up but fell backwards with the severed ends of the blades in her hand.

"Come on!" John shouted into the wind which was curling the fog around them.

She took the spoon from her pocket and frantically dug around the base of the clump trying to loosen it from the home it had inhabited for decades. Her hands were damp, freezing and sore and the spoon had bent under the strain, but she continued to stab at the stubborn roots until she thought she had loosened the edges. She threw the spoon aside and curled both hands around the large tuft, dug her heels between clumps of heather and pulled. The momentum as it finally lost the battle sent her backwards with a thump where she sat with the huge clump of grass and almost a foot of soil and roots in her hand.

"What the hell!" John was not amused.

Quickly she dropped the pot into the void and dropped the clump back into its rightful place before stamping on it and making her way back to John who she suspected might be having second thoughts about the whole situation.

Gingerly she opened her bag and took out a bottle of red wine and two glasses wrapped in a hotel hand towel. He looked at her for a moment and then laughed. Immediately she felt relief.

"You never fail to astonish me!" he smiled, "it's freezing up here, the fogs coming in fast and you want to drink wine!"

She handed him the towel and wedged the stems of the glasses in the snow.

He opened the towel and laid it gently on a grassy outcrop.

"Be seated mi lady." He gave it so easily!

She sat down with a thump and poured the wine knowing that they were alright again. To the west, the orange sun was about to disappear over the horizon and as she poured the wine, she leaned against him for warmth and support. She knew these were two of the many things she would rely on him for in the years to come if she could hold onto him long enough. She drank in the moment which was as rich and aromatic as the wine on her lips. This was a moment she would remember in her old age when she could tell their grandchildren of the little time capsule that may never be found up on the eerie mountain which was the start of the great love of their Grandma and Granddad. She smiled, then turned to John who seemed to have been jumpstarted into the mischievous rogue she first met.

"Let's make love." He was tugging awkwardly at his trousers with frozen fingers.

"You are joking?"

"Do I look like I am?"

It was her turn to be shocked, but she was not going to be the party pooper and started to pull off one of her boots to enable her to take one leg out of her ski pants. He was on top of her within seconds fumbling with clothing until he put his hand over her mouth to quieten her.

"Shh I can hear something."

Voices in the distance were getting nearer as they lay perfectly still while the last group of seasoned hikers thudded past them on the track only a few yards away. The heat from their bodies was melting the snow and Sophies back was already wet through her jacket.

She was still listening to the fading voices when he entered her. It took her breath so completely she could hardly exhale from that first thrust of pleasure. The silence was replaced by gasps of exertion as they pushed against each other with equal effort. The hand that had been silencing her mouth fell clumsily, now pressing into her face causing her to catch breaths through his huge fingers. He was oblivious to anything other than his approaching orgasm while the cold wetness beneath her, the weight of his body crushing her, and the hand causing her to fight for each breath, accelerated her pleasure until they met in a wave of simultaneous release.

He dropped limply on top of her forcing her to try to scramble from underneath him to take the breaths she desperately needed.

"I'm sorry." he puffed between his own bids for air.

"Don't apologise," she laughed, "just move, you're crushing me again."

"That's what you get when you fall for a fatty." he teased pulling her to her feet and kissing her firmly, "I'm an eternal frigging teenager with you."

"I hope that never changes." She closed her eyes as the warmth of another kiss thawed her lips.

The descent was more difficult than the ascent as they skidded, slipped and stumbled in complete darkness down the icy path with the vision of a warm bath and fresh white linen sheets beckoning.

In contrast to the hurried and passionate encounters of the car, beach and mountain side, that night, after they had bathed and wrapped themselves in hotel bathrobes, he made love to her gently and slowly. She didn't want the night to end – not ever. It was not the romantic notion of a lovesick girl but the deepest fear at what the end of the night might deliver.

"Let's get some sleep." He said kissing her on the forehead.

Gently she slid backwards until she felt the warmth of his chest against her back and his protective arm slide sleepily around her waist. She stroked the course hairs on his forearm and allowed herself to indulge in this moment of protection from her man. The man she loved with all her heart. The man who made her feel like a woman while Carl had only ever made her feel like a girl. Slowly she wrapped her arm around his in the hope that this would provide an anchor to keep her in his world, in this world, in their world

She lay awake for hours. If she lost this moment, she felt she may as well die. She wanted to die rather than lose John and the darkest of thoughts started to creep into her mind, niggling and suggesting, terrifying and haunting her.

She was living a double life, and no-one was able to help her or even to understand it. She didn't know much about anything but laying there with John beside her on the eve or their new life, one thing was certain. It had to stop. It had to stop, and she was the only one who could do it.

She recalled the night in the pub with Niki and Kelly. She recalled Kelly's reaction when she had declared she wanted a love to die for. "You want something that would make you feel so wretched?"

She recalled the guy who had been trying to recover from such a love for years, living proof that there was no cure for something that truly takes your heart.

Amidst these ramblings of despair and determination, an idea came to her. An idea so terrifying that she could feel the prickles of sweat glands secreting tiny globules of moisture over her entire body. A fear of her own intentions, a terror of herself – almost like there was a second self to be reckoned with. A second self who had concluded that if she ever found herself back in the world without John, she would kill herself in the hope that it would leave her only one existence. This one. Forever.

She tried to silence the obsessed person inside her, to reason with the irrational being who was slowly but surely fighting for control.

Would she really face death for the uncertain and unlikely possibility that she might keep John forever? She turned to look at him, sleeping peacefully beside her, right where he belonged, and she knew the answer.

Just as certainly as her resolve had been broken on her trip to the vending machine, just as certainly as her false bargain with God, she knew she could not live without this man.

But fear gripped her once again and angrily and forcefully she drove the idea back down to the darkness from where it had risen. She made herself a promise that she would never think of it again, reassuring herself that the idea had been a moment of insanity, a seed of madness, yet the seed had been sewn and deep inside her soul it was being nurtured by her other self. By her potential murderer.

Chapter 13

She was still in the same position when she woke up. She had been nudged from slumber by a stirring from behind. She smiled as she nestled backwards towards him teasingly. He slid an arm around her and pressed gently on her stomach to hold her in place as he slid his erection between her thighs.

She smiled and made a small gasp as he entered her, closing her eyes to savour the moment of this morning greeting. But something didn't feel right. His scent, his body weight behind those gentle thrusts, the sound of his breathing. Horrific tiny pieces of the same dreadful jigsaw were slotting together, enlightening her as slowly and surely as the sun creeps over a shaded garden. Gradually and cruelly revealing once again the portrait of hell. This was Carl inside her! This was Carl, and John was gone. Once again cruelly ejected from her life, back into the unknown.

She froze as he started to thrust more purposefully, hardly noticing the act at all, as she tried to rewind to where she had left life with Carl in her parents' house. Ambivalence gave way to disappointment, but disappointment grew rapidly to resentment and resentment exploded into anger. Anger that Carl would think of relieving himself at all amidst her grief and worry for her mother.

She remained perfectly still in an attempt to negate her previous gesture of encouragement. His pace quickened and he seemed oblivious to the lack of participation on her part. She wanted to spin around and slap him, but she knew she was on shaky ground. She had teased him, accidentally mistaking him for another man, and that granted him an infuriating pardon. So, she gritted her teeth and dug her nails into the pillow so hard she could feel them bending painfully against her own flesh.

Carl was gasping and grunting as he neared orgasm and she could feel the sweat from his body touching her buttocks. She closed her eyes tightly and counted in her head until she felt him convulse against her back and fall limply away from her.

As he recovered, he put his arm back around her, but she was still gripping the pillow, hardly breathing as the tears were forced through her tightly closed eyes. She pressed her tongue hard onto the roof of her mouth to stifle the sob that was threatening to draw attention to her misery.

"You ok?" At last Carl had resumed conscious thought.

She didn't speak for a moment. An interrogation from Carl was the last thing she wanted to face right now, so she swallowed hard to control the tears and spoke as confidently as she could.

"Yes love, just a bit tired."

He seemed content with her explanation and cuddled up as she cringed again.

They lay silently for a moment, listening to her father on the telephone.

"It sounds like the hospital on the phone." Carl said yawning.

Sophie tried to sound appropriately concerned, but she had just left a place where her mum was healthy and full of life.

She stared blankly at the familiar ice cream swirls of aertex which had infiltrated every room of this house in the eighties and now looked impossible to ever remove. There was no longer any emotion in her heart. Emotion had become too exhausting and had been replaced with defeated acceptance of the situation and a futile yearning that everything in her life could be as steadfast as the aertex above her.

Carl slid out of her, leaving an annoying dribble down her leg, but she couldn't be bothered to do anything about that either. She was about to start another day in a world where nothing made sense or seemed to matter to her anymore. She would go through the motions, just as she always did and pray for this nightmare to end soon, very soon.

She made her way downstairs in the oversized tee shirt she had slept in and the sticky dampness of Carl rubbing between her thighs with every step. Her father was at the table looking blankly out of the window. She bid him good morning but there was no response at all. His eyes were fixed and emotionless, his complexion sickly green.

"What' the matter?" She rubbed his hand gently to command his attention.

He turned his head and looked at her as though he had never seen her before.

"Dad?"

"The operation was a disaster."

"Disaster? What does that mean?"

"They couldn't remove the tumour because it's grown into other parts of her brain and attached itself to an artery."

"So, what are they going to do?" Sophie feared she already knew the answer.

"I don't know. We need to go and see her."

Sophie wanted to put her arms around him but held back. Sympathy felt like defeat and dad desperately needed hope. They needed to stay strong and positive.

"They can do all kinds of things without operating dad. It doesn't mean she's out of options."

"I know love." He squeezed her hand and smiled, protecting her in the same way that she was trying to protect him, as Carl clattered down the stairs into the kitchen. He had obviously caught most of the conversation.

"I'll run you both in." He was already reaching for his keys.

"No. It's fine," Sophie barked. She didn't want him anywhere near her this morning and she definitely didn't want him smothering her in unwelcome affection.

"We can take dad's car. I'll drive. There's no point in you missing work. This is Friday, right?"

"Yes, it's Friday but I don't mind taking the day off."

"No!" She snapped harshly "Dad and I need to spend some time together on this."

It was an unmistakeable slap in the face. An exclusion from the family he was meant to be a part of, but under the circumstance she had the perfect vindication. Carl would cut her some slack, believing the words to be born of panic and grief for her mother, not from disgust and anger that he had just tricked her into betraying the lover she yearned for.

Her disposition mellowed as she got into the driver's seat and helped her father fasten the seatbelt that his shaking hands couldn't seem to align. The journey passed in silence. Grief was premature, comfort out of reach, and hope seemed like evaporating particles of moisture they were powerless to contain.

They had never been a religious family, but they were among the millions who disallowed themselves to dismiss it out loud just in case 'he' was listening, causing them to be duly damned. In the hypocrisy of desperation, she prayed as she stared through the windscreen which was undoubtedly taking her closer and closer to certain heartbreak. She asked for forgiveness, apologised for all the times she had ridiculed religion. Prayed for a second chance. For her mother's life. Then she prayed for something else, she prayed that one of these worlds would disappear forever. She prayed that it would be this one.

As she drove into the hospital carpark, it felt like time was running out. She couldn't wait around for her prayers to be answered. If this world was to disappear, she knew she, was the one who probably had the power to make it happen. She asked God for a sign even though he was unlikely to manifest himself in the grounds of Scarborough hospital.

Her thoughts turned back to John. She wondered if he was still sleeping with his arms around her or if he had woken this morning to find her gone. Perhaps he was loading up his shiny red sports car with the crisp littered carpets and wondering why she had abandoned him. She suddenly gripped the steering wheel…... Red! His car was red, and he had been wearing a blue sweater!! She could remember the colours of her last day with John even down to the pink floral tablecloths in the hotel restaurant. She remembered the bitterness of the coffee that made her wish she had ordered tea instead. Her life with John was real and, as she pulled on the handbrake, she was sure that this was her sign. This was the God she didn't believe in, telling her that this was the world she shouldn't believe in.

She smiled. It didn't matter anymore how ill her mother was because she knew she had the power to change things. To eradicate the tears in her father's eyes along with the memory of them, but for now she would comfort him, and she held onto his arm with renewed faith and a lighter heart as they made their way to the ward.

Gently she held her mother's hand and tried to dispel the fear in the eyes that had comforted her throughout her life. She could see the terror, and there was nothing anyone could say to console her. The unspoken thoughts were written boldly on the face of everyone around her. Doctors and nurses mirrored one another's weak smiles and extended the same futile comfort of placing their hands on top of hers as though this would somehow help to dilute her fear and sorrow.

The person who had comforted and protected her all her life, who had taught her never to give up, was now defeated. Behind those gentle eyes there was no determination to fight, only the dignified acceptance that this was not a battle she could win.

"I'm dying, aren't I?" Finally, she asked softly as though trying to keep the secret from her husband.

Sophie couldn't speak for the lump in her throat and she didn't know how to answer this question even if she had the power to speak.

She stroked her mum's shaved pitiful head over the dried blood and swelling where her skull had been sawn open. It was more than she could bear.

"I am, aren't I? Sophie love?"

"I don't know mum. No-one has told us anything."

She squeezed Sophie's hand and then kissed it.

"I think I am dying, from what the doctor said earlier."

"Why? What did he say?"

"Nothing much, but it was the way he avoided telling me about any planned treatment or any more surgery. It was written all over his face."

Sophie turned to her father for inspiration, but he was shaking, and his face was turned away, so instead she looked down at the floor. This feeling of total helplessness was consuming her. She wanted to run home and go asleep so she could wake up where her mum was fine, and her dad was happy again. She wanted to stay awake for ever in that world and never return to this one.

The voice of the person she feared was becoming louder again. The voice from within, rising up and daring her to consider that she could choose one of these lives by ending the other permanently.

She tried to dismiss it. To reassure herself that she could never be convinced to do it, but her comforting promises felt fragile. Her heartbeat was already quickening from fear of the other voice and the undeniable fact from which she couldn't hide….. her murderer was pacing.

She shuddered and took her dad's hand.

"I'm going to find a doctor."

He nodded and sat down beside the frail remnants of what had once been his rosy-cheeked, glamorous, vibrant wife.

Sophie eventually managed a few moments with the busy consultant who had the manners and appearance of a college student.

"I'm sorry." he said as though he had accidentally bumped into her.

"Sorry?" she frowned "for what?"

"Has no-one explained the situation?"

"Not really. Other than the fact that the operation didn't go to plan"

"We explained it all to your father on the phone this morning." he sighed condescendingly as though his time was being wasted.

"Well, I don't think my dad was in the right frame of mind to take in whatever you told him, do you? More to the point, why did you tell him over the phone if it was bad news?"

"Look" he was clearly irritated by Sophie's audacity to challenge him "I asked him to come in, but he insisted so I tried to explain the situation"

"So, what does that mean? What exactly is the situation?"

"The reality is, that all we can offer now is palliative care."

"So that's it? You're just giving up on her?"

"I'm sorry." He repeated with a touch more empathy than previously. His pager went off and he was gone.

She stood there for a moment, absorbing the facts, absorbing the reality of what lay ahead and then absorbing the image in front of her. Her dad sat resignedly on his plastic chair trying to offer some degree of comfort when there was none to be had.

She couldn't bear it. More importantly, she didn't intend to. The voice she had been drowning out was now louder than her own and she no longer feared it. The entity she had been slamming the door on was now being welcomed with open arms and as she marched back towards her dying mother, this inner person became her accomplice.

"It's ok mum. You are going to be fine. You are not going to die. I promise." She handed her dad twenty pounds "I need to go. Here, take a taxi."

She didn't wait for either of them to speak as she kissed them both and headed out of the hospital. Emotion overwhelmed her as she made her way through the maze of corridors and swinging doors, guided by the signs that were now blurred by tears. She strode purposefully as she committed to walking out of this hospital, out of this nightmare, out of this world and back to her own world ....permanently.

She was going to destroy this version of her life and make sure that fate, or whatever this phenomenon was, could not interfere again. She was going to return to the man she loved and her healthy mother and live a contented life and nothing was going to stop her. She had a head start as she knew her dad would stay most of the day with her mum. He was probably intending to stay by her side until forcibly removed.

She drove back to her parents' home and searched the cabinet where he kept his Christmas alcohol. On opening it, the smell was exactly as she remembered it when she used to sneak into it for a glass of sherry as a teenager. She pulled out a bottle of Vodka and stood it on the table while she went upstairs for her sleeping pills. In the bathroom cabinet she found painkillers and returned to place them all beside the Vodka. So, there it was. Her escape plan. Her ticket to a new life.

Affectionately she cradled the elements in her arms hoping that together they had the strength, for between them they had to transport her back into John's arms. As she put the key in the rickety door of the garden shed, she caught a glimpse of her reflection in the glass. There was no fear at facing her murderer, none at all.

One by one she popped the pills into her mouth and washed each down with a gulp from the bottle. There was no turning back now, she had no intention of waking up with an almighty hangover, so she needed to keep up the momentum before the Vodka had chance to impair her ability to finish the job. She drank and swallowed and drank and swallowed gulping the fiery liquid evenly and consistently.

She was almost at the end of the bottle and all the pills had gone but her body had not yet caught up and her presence of mind was not adequately impaired. She started to panic. There were a few agonising moments when she realised that, without immediate help, she was already dead, and in a few moments, would be incapable of calling for any. For these few moments, moments when it felt like she still had a choice she flew into a blind panic.

She forced her fingers down her throat in an attempt to vomit but the ringing in her ears was deafening and as double vision gave way to multiple vision, she tried to hold herself up by the handle of the vice on her dad's oil-stained bench. He had taught her how to make a jewellery box with that vice, how proud and grown up she had felt at being allowed to use his tools.

She was now sweating with fear as she gripped the cold steel and her eyes could no longer focus at all. She could feel that it was too late now, and the end was near. She felt her head hit the workbench with a sickening crack before feeling the damp wooden floor. She could smell the damp musty wood only inches from her nostrils and feel the trickle of blood, hot as tea, pouring over her face into her ear, somewhere in the distance there was the fading squawk of gulls until the ringing in her ears drowned them out.

She tried desperately to stay awake and made a second futile attempt to thrust her fingers into her mouth, but she could hardly raise her hand from the cold floor. Her eyes closed slowly until she was alone with her thoughts, with her soul, with her God.

She prayed once again as the arms of the angels seemed to engulf her cold poisoned body and fold her into the warmth and softness of their wings. She heard her own breathing become shallow and her heartbeat slow until the gap between each beat was so long, she was waiting for each one to confirm she was still alive. While waiting for one such beat, she hoped that it was almost over. If this was dying then at least there was no pain to it, the ringing had gone and as she slowly reopened her eyes, she could just make out enough to establish that the double vision was no more.

In death she was still lying on her side but feeling very little other than a new warmth. She tried to move her arm, expecting to have no control over it, but she lifted it quite easily. Gently and slowly she felt behind her, trying to connect to the divine being which was holding her so comfortingly.

"Good morning sexy."

Chapter 14

She froze with her hand resting on chest hair.

"John?"

"Who else would it be?"

She took a deep breath and then smiled widely, whispering 'thank you' to the God that had answered her prayer. She had done it! She had finally done it and now her life could start again, here with John.

She buried her head in his chest and breathed him in deeply.

"Don't ever leave me." It was a plea from the heart, but she was asking something of him that he could never understand nor probably control.

"I will try."

"No. Promise me."

"I can't promise, anything could happen."

She knew he was right, but she also knew he didn't appreciate how much she needed that promise.

She got out of the soft scented sheets and pulled back the curtains to reveal the view of the snow-covered mountain they had climbed only the night before.

She knew in her heart, that tonight there would be no fear when she closed her eyes. She would sleep soundly in the certainty that she would wake up beside John and she would continue to do so for the rest of her life. After all, there was now nothing to go back to. This life was the only place she existed, and she was going to grasp happiness with both hands.

"I'm going to call my mum today and tell her the wedding is off".

He didn't comment. It seemed respectful to remain silent and she appreciated that sometimes there are statements to which silence is the appropriate response.

She picked up her phone and took it into the privacy of the bathroom to break the news but was both shocked and elated by her mother's reaction.

"Well. These things happen love and we just want you to be happy. Better to find out now than later. Can't argue with love"

It was a collection of clichés that almost made it amusing. It reminded her of the many clichés her mother recited when she was a child. Such as 'least said soonest mended' or 'many a true word spoken in jest' She seemed to have one for every occasion, but these must have been saved up especially for today.

"Thanks mum."

"For what?"

"For not going mad at me."

"Well, no good crying over spilt milk."

Sophie stifled a giggle and said goodbye.

She returned to the bedroom where John was flicking over the TV channels.

"How was it?"

"I'm not really sure it sank in. She just accepted it like I had told her I had taken a dress back to a shop. It's like she didn't understand or something."

"Maybe she is going lala." He faked a shudder.

Sophie panicked "What made you say that?"

"I was joking." He frowned .

"There's nothing wrong with her mind."

"Ok ok! I was only joking!"

She kissed him an apology and he kissed her back, a little warily.

She noticed his apprehension and made a mental note to stop drawing attention to herself like this. She wondered if one day there would be no secrets between them. If she would tell him about her problem, her loss of grip on reality, her mad dreams. It was her turn to shudder.

They packed up the car again and headed back down the icy lane to continue their journey to London. As they neared the end of the M11 she started to ask more questions about his life there, his apartment, job and friends. She had no need to collate this kind of information anymore, but it was a habit she found difficult to break.

As the car pulled into the designated parking spot outside his high-rise apartment block, she watched a plane landing on the runway of the City of London airport. The building was impressive, vast expanses of glass frontage and a large reception area. She followed him into the lift and waited while he selected the floor, number 11. She made another needless mental note and slipped her hand round him under his jacket. He smoothed her hair from her face and spoke softly.

"Welcome home lover."

She smiled and pressed herself more closely to him. It felt like one of those moments she would recall many times over many years and for that reason she wanted to savour it, smell it, feel it and as it's perfection gently unfolded, she committed it to memory as the lift jerked into motion.

If John had felt like home at first sight, then the apartment certainly didn't. It was clinical, mostly white or cream and there were no carpets over the tiles, no ornaments or photographs, no pictures or colour. So different from the flat she had shared with Carl which was cluttered with memorabilia and sentimental trinkets. For the first time since meeting John, she felt an emptiness. Her heart was sinking but she knew she was just feeling like a stranger in this place and that it wouldn't be long before this sterile dwelling bore her stamp on it.

While she was still battling with her sunken heart and home sickness, he had watched the joy draining from her face and quickly scooped her up in his arms swirling her around.

"Come here Mrs Cardwell."

It was exactly what she needed to hear as he transported her into the bedroom and kissed her with the passion that always stole her breath for a moment. This was the certainty she had come to believe in, and today it would not leave even a crack where any doubt could creep in. She was home.

"I'm no-one's wife yet, you know."

"Yes, I know."

It was the perfect moment for a proposal but instead he pulled her into the bedroom, already trying to unbutton his shirt.

The next few days were like a small holiday from life itself.

John went to work on the DLR every day and Sophie played house. She shopped and cleaned and cooked for John and tried to pretend that this was forever. Each night she cooked two different meals just so they could cut everything in half and perform the swapping ceremony which always set the mood of fun and sharing – in her mind it had become a good luck ritual.

Every morning when she awoke, fear gripped her for a few moments until she verified exactly where she was and that she had not wandered between worlds during the night. She didn't contact Kelly or Niki at all. She didn't want anything to break this spell. It would be broken soon enough, and for now she wanted to enjoy the utopia of spending the days making her home and herself look wonderful and the evenings sharing romantic dinners with John.

Afterwards she would perch on his lap at the window and take in the view of London while sipping red wine, chatting and laughing in this time bubble they had created.

She sent her letter of resignation to work and covered the shortfall with a sick note for stress convincing herself that there was little left to deal with from her past. From time to time a voice in her subconscious tried to point out that her life seemed too perfect to be true, but she abruptly dismissed it and violently reprimanded it for trying to spoil things.

She prayed every night for her sanity to remain intact and as the days passed, she became more and more confident that her period of madness was now over. This was her way of rationalising the disturbing events, yet the rebellious voice still nagged quietly, asking her to explain how this new sanity could have been caused by a suicide in a make-believe world. The question was as unsettling as this perfect love, but she was not going to spoil the joy she was feeling by poking holes in its credibility.

As the days turned to weeks, the outside world started to nudge them with increasing frequency until eventually they had to acknowledge that there were things to be done.

"You need to go back and tie up the loose ends Sophie."

"I know." She sighed in the same way she used to when she'd been reprimanded for leaving her homework until the last day of the holidays.

"If you make a list of what needs to be done, we can keep the trip to a minimum."

"You don't need to come with me John, I can sort this myself."

"But you need to finish the cancellation of the wedding plans for your mum. You said you wanted to see Niki and Kelly again, pick up the rest of your things from the flat and clear your desk from work. You need a car to transport it all."

"Really John. I'll be fine. There are only a few clothes to pick up and some documents and hopefully my car is still there to bring it back. I'll take the train up there. I would rather do this myself."

"If you are sure?"

"Yup. My mess. I'll sort it"

John shrugged but didn't argue.

Collecting the remainder of her possessions from the flat was something she had been dreading, and although she would have loved to see Niki again, she had decided from the cool telephone conversations that it really wasn't a good idea. She knew only too well that it's practically impossible not to take sides when a couple you are very close to, break up and it had become glaringly obvious that Niki and Pete had taken Carl's.

She didn't mind too much, as she was thankful that he had people to support him, but there was still a heavy sadness over this lost friendship.

Kelly had surprisingly been more receptive to keeping in touch. She was grateful for the lack of judgmental behaviour even though it was likely that Kelly just didn't have the energy for moral high ground. It meant that she could at least call in on the Saturday afternoon for coffee before making her trip to their old flat and probably to some sort of confrontation with Carl.

After two changeovers the train sped along into the familiar scenery of the Yorkshire countryside and finally into the station of her hometown. She travelled with a small overnight case for her stay at her parents and hoped that her old sports bag and suitcase would still be at the flat for her return journey. She had prepared herself mentally for the task ahead. Decided that there was no room for emotion or sentimental trips down memory lane with Carl. She wanted nothing from the flat other than clothes and a few treasured items from her childhood. The sooner she got on with it the sooner she could return to John and pick up her new life in the city.

She made her way through the station towards the taxi rank wearing casual canvas trousers, a baggy sweatshirt and a waterproof over jacket. She had chosen carefully so as not to appear like she was rubbing Carl's nose in this, she was also hoping to discourage any temptation he may have to try to win her back. She had captured her hair in a messy loose side plait which she hoped looked more unkempt than sexy or wanton. Only a touch of lip-gloss and a little mascara, no perfume.

As the taxi pulled up outside Kelly's she could see her friend at the window in obvious anticipation, and before she reached the door it flew open and she was being hugged breathless.

"Wow" She croaked.

"I'm so pleased to see you Soph" Kelly was surprisingly emotional.

"You too." Sophie choked. This was a sudden rush of emotion she hadn't expected Kelly to trigger.

Kelly was exactly as expected with her perfect French Pleat, heavy face makeup, shaped eyebrows, painted and glossed lips and false eyelashes lined perfectly to conceal the join. Her pink sheer slacks were too dressy for a normal Saturday morning and her silk blouse followed her curves seamlessly over a carefully chosen smooth and neutral tee shirt bra. Kelly's attention to detail was remarkable.

Even though the hug had ended Kelly had held onto Sophie's hand in an affectionate way.

"Is everything alright Kelly?"

"No or course not. My friend has moved to London." She smiled weakly.

Sophie had never really considered herself to be this close to Kelly but now it seemed that as Niki had deserted her, and Kelly had stepped up to the mark in a way she hadn't expected. She squeezed Kelly's hand in an unspoken thank you.

"So how are you and are you seeing anyone?"

"Yes, I am" Kelly smiled "He's lovely."

"Lovely?" What is he? a cupcake?"

"I like him."

"Like?"

"Yes, I like him and he's lovely. That's perfect for me."

"Really?"

"Yup. You know me. I don't have the energy for lust, fireworks, tantrums and tears. I'm going for calm, nice, predictable and safe. Contentment. That's what real happiness is made of, no pain and no heartache!"

"Yes, I remember that safe predictability. Is that enough for you? It wasn't enough for me."

"So, you think this shit storm you are living in is so much better?" Her eyes were widening "a flat miles away from your family and friends, no job, your dad's money down the drain and a really nice guy trying to pick up the pieces of a shattered life? Is that the dream for you?"

"I'm fine." Sophie snapped trying to hide the impact of so many truthful missiles.

"You are at the moment, but I doubt it will last."

"You don't know that. I love John in a way you will never understand. You may be willing to settle for something less than love but I'm not, and I will get a job and I will also get new friends." She knew instantly that she had overstepped the mark. Kelly was her childhood friend and that's a special bond she could never replace. She tried to take it back.

"I didn't mean…"

"Don't say any more," Kelly's eyes were misty with tears "this is not like you. These words are not coming from my friend. This John has changed you, and not for the better."

Sophie felt irritated but she decided to leave it and change the conversation. Kelly wasn't letting it go.

"I'm trying to protect you Soph. I have seen what this whirlwind, passionate, fantasy kind of infatuation can do. The havoc it can wreak and the devastation it can leave in its wake."

"I don't know what you mean?"

"You know my parents broke up when I was about ten?"

Sophie nodded. She did remember but it was all a bit vague probably because it didn't really make much difference to her at the time. The only change seemed to be that Kelly and her sister got more freedom when they suddenly had only their mum to contend with. The only other change was that there were some weekends when they couldn't play because they were at their father's house. It didn't really seem much of a deal at the time.

"My mum and dad were childhood sweethearts. They were dating at fourteen. Mum knew even then that he was the one. she told us all the time that finding the one person who you just know will never let you down is the most real, wonderful and certain feeling in the world. She told us never to settle for anything less than true love. Then suddenly – wham – the love of her life was the subject of someone else's true love."

"Oh, I didn't know," Sophie tried to inject some empathy into her voice, but she was irritated by the moral of this story, "he fell in love with another woman?"

"No. That's the worst thing about this. I don't think he did. Some other woman fell in love with him in the same desperate, all-consuming way and she set out to get him with her irresistible charm, her unlimited budget for fancy clothes, hair and makeup. Her witty conversation and untiring enthusiasm for his interests. She made him feel wanted and interesting. She made his old life look mundane and boring in comparison. She was cleverly competing with someone who didn't even know she was being scored. Mum didn't have a chance. He had an affair, mum found out and for her it was broken"

"But if she loved him and he loved her then surely she could forgive him?"

"Yes, she forgave him. She still loved him, but the trust had gone. She couldn't feel that wonderful certain feeling again and she didn't feel the same loyalty to him either. Their love was still there but they couldn't live it. They could see it but not touch it. Mum said it was like grieving for him as though he had died but she could still see him through a glass door. Neither of them ever loved again. This all-consuming love they shared destroyed them and spoiled them for anyone else. Nothing could measure up to it- nothing could bring it back. You see, they still only wanted each other even though it was too late. Awful."

"But your dad married again?"

"No, he didn't. He moved in with his new woman, but they argued all the time. He blamed her for losing us, his family and his home but mostly I think he blamed her for destroying the love he'd felt in his marriage. Sadly, this stupid woman still loved him, and she took his wrath and put up with his anger. She got a broken man. There were no winners."

Sophie listened in silence and wondered if she had in some way scarred Carl and made him lose faith in love. She hoped not. She hoped he didn't love her that much. She couldn't speak for several minutes as she absorbed Kelly's story. She was shocked that Kelly with her superficial ambience was actually the deepest and most emotional of all of them. So sensitive that she had hit the shutdown button early in life to spare herself from the horror she knew her own heart could create should she allow it to run free.

"Penny for them." Kelly said more cheerfully.

"I think you know them already." Sophie replied with a deep sigh.

"Do you want me to come with you?"

"Would you?"

"Of course." Kelly squeezed her hand.

Once again Sophie was taken aback by Kelly's warmth as she returned the squeeze and smiled.

"Come on let's get this over with then we can come back here, and I'll cook for us before you go to your mum's" Kelly was already reaching for her coat. Sophie pulled on her trainers and picked up her jacket, taking a deep breath to steal herself for the ordeal ahead.

"We'll be back before you know it."

Sophie nodded and held open the door.

Chapter 15

Walking to Kelly's car, she noticed that spring was starting to make an appearance, with tiny green buds on the bushes, even though it was only March. This was the time when everyone starts to feel more positive about life and Sophie felt sure Carl would be feeling it too. Making a new start and a new life for himself and she wished him all the best from the bottom of her heart. Maybe he already had a girlfriend. Remarkably she felt nothing at all about the idea, other than it would be a weight lifted, how differently she felt now from the jealousy she had felt when she heard of his millennium kiss with the girl from work only a few months ago.

The little car twisted and turned the short journey to her old flat and as Kelly pulled on the handbrake on the street outside, they could both see Carl's car parked outside in its usual spot.

"You want me to come in with you?"

"No thanks. If he has an audience, he may play to it. You know what a man's ego is like. I need to do this on my own. I owe him that much."

She walked purposefully towards the communal door and rang his bell, noticing that it still had both their names on the handwritten slip of paper slotted behind the tiny plastic window. She remembered the excitement of writing that label and having to poke it in without crumpling the flimsy bit of paper because she couldn't wait until they could buy card. She rang the bell and waited for a few moments before ringing it again and peering through the glass panel at the stairway inside. There was no sign of him, but she could hear music playing upstairs and tried to decide if it was appropriate to use her key or not.

She didn't want to do anything to annoy him as there were some delicate matters to discuss, and the one at the forefront of her mind was her share of the money in their joint account. It was the money they had been saving for a deposit on a house and a few weeks ago she had resolved to let him have it. There had been that moment of morality when she felt he deserved everything, and she should leave with nothing but as the weeks passed and the last of her wages were gobbled up by the cost of London living, she had nothing left and still no job.

Of course, John would support her but being his incumbent burden was not part of her plan nor was it the image she wanted to portray. When they had met, she was on the brink of a promising career and supporting herself was something she needed for her self-esteem, for her self-respect, for her ego.

She didn't want John to think less of her, but the truth was that she was afraid of even the smallest decline in his lust and love for her. She needed the money she and Carl had skimped and scraped to put away for their first home. She told herself she needed it to pay her way but deep down she also knew the shameful truth was that she needed it to squander on luxuries and outfits to impress her new man.

She saw Kelly frowning at the length of time she had stood outside and waved to let her know everything was fine. Realising that she had been dilly dallying, she slipped the key in the lock and pushed open the door with new resolve. The money was rightfully hers and she could do whatever she liked with it. She would just be careful on how she approached the matter.

As she climbed the stairs, she could tell that the music was his radio and the fact that he was playing it on full volume meant that he was most likely decorating. Probably painting her out of the flat and clearing the way for his new life. She didn't blame him but the thought of it did hurt in an unexpected way. She didn't want to be so brutally obliterated and the relief she thought she would feel at him moving on failed to emerge. Perhaps she at least wanted him to mourn her loss more gently and slowly than to erase her with a paintbrush and deafening music.

At the top of the stairs, she banged loudly on the door in the hope he could hear her above the noise. He didn't answer but she wasn't surprised as she could hardly hear the knock herself. She knocked once more and then used her second key and gently pushed open the door to their kitchen.

"Carl?"

There was no answer.

"Carl, it's me, Sophie."

Still nothing. She started to feel uneasy and thought about leaving. Something didn't feel right. She suspected he had seen her car and might be lying in wait for her or perhaps he had another woman here. She looked nervously at the bedroom door. She imagined that if she opened it, he might pounce on her and pin her to the wall, inflicting his anger on her, spitting insults into her face or she might open it to see him making love in their bed to the woman who would take her place. The woman who might steal her wedding and watch him play cup matches on Saturdays with dinner cooking the way she used to. Suddenly she didn't feel good about anything.

She was being stupid. This was Carl and he was the gentlest and most faithful man she knew. It was more likely he had left the music on and gone out for a run or was having one of his never-ending showers where he couldn't hear a thing. She was the one who always went around switching everything off. She smiled a little as she remembered this trait had sometimes found its way onto her list of pros and cons. How long ago all that felt now.

She could probably get all her things without even having to confront him.

Gently she nudged the door. She couldn't see anyone, so she pushed a little harder. The door swung back at her as though something was behind it. Her uneasiness turned to fear as she again imagined Carl standing in wait. Surely not. She forced herself to dismiss the idea and pushed the door again, this time squeezing through the small gap it allowed. The moment she popped out at the other side it flew back out of her hand as a heavy weight hit her from behind. She spun around into the huge object which swung against her, covering her face with its cold dampness. Two bare feet dangled at her waist. She opened her mouth to scream but no sound came out and her feet refused to move though she tried with all her might to communicate with them.

Terror gripped her entire body as the horror before her seeped slowly into her conscious mind. A bloated face starred down at her with bloodshot bulging eyes. Grey in colour, contorted from the neck, swollen like a balloon, tongue lolling grotesquely from blue blood-stained lips. There were smears of blood all over the wall. Inside she was screaming over and over but there was still no sound. The pink striped shirt swinging back and forth above her head was the one she had bought at Christmas. This was Carl! She tried to take his weight as she screamed at the top of her voice but the music from the radio absorbed her voice into its happy beat seamlessly.

"I'm sorry. Oh God! I'm so sorry. You'll be ok." Her frantic, desperate, wasted words were drowned by the cruel ill-fated rhythm of the Spice Girls. She tried with all her might to hold his weight with her arms clasped around his urine-soaked legs. The weight of him was unbearable, her body was shaking with the strain, but she held fast, using every molecule of her body's strength in a bid to keep him in in this world, praying out loud over and over for him to take a breath. Her desperation was beyond reason. She could feel that his body was cold, the stench in her face told her that the urine was still damp but stale, his legs were stiff like those of a shop manakin. He had been dead for some time but the superhuman effort came from a need deep inside her.

The pain she was feeling in every muscle of her body was nothing more than penance born of guilt, a futile plea for redemption for the pain she had inflicted, but there was no-one to witness her effort other than the God she had so recently started to acknowledge, just in case. This was not an attempt to save Carl, it was a penitent display of remorse, aimed at negating any reprisal that might otherwise come her way.

Slowly and gently, she allowed her arms to relax as she looked up at the repulsive swollen bulge of flesh that had once been his face. His body dropped heavily from her arms, the head bouncing on its flaccid neck like a balloon in a child's hand. Vomit was oozing from her own mouth, down onto her sweatshirt but she had no recollection of retching it from her stomach.

Slowly she walked to the door, down the stairs, onto the street and sat on the pavement with the stench of her own vomit and

Carl's stale urine in her hair, on her clothes and drying on her face. She felt Kelly's arms around her and watched her frantic face mouthing words she couldn't hear. Questions she couldn't answer, until she was physically pulled from the ground and guided back up the stairs to return to the spectacle she had just escaped. Numbed by shock and despair she obediently climbed each step, re-opened the door to the bedroom and watched blankly as Kelly looked up at the horror above, made no futile attempt to save him and dialled 999 with shaking hands.

Sophie starred at the floor and as Kelly spoke to the emergency operator, she spotted two folded sheets of paper. Both had concertina like folds as though they had been held firmly in a hand. They were directly beneath his body and it was obvious he had been holding them. One she recognised immediately as the note she had left for Carl as she saw a few words in her own handwriting, the other had her name clearly visible on the outer fold. Her grief gave way to self-preservation as she quickly swept them both up and stuffed them in the pocket of her canvas walking pants. She needed to remove anything that might further incriminate her morally to this tragedy. She had enough enemies. Kelly shot her a reprimanding glance amid her conversation with the Police department. She had seen. She knew it was hiding evidence. She continued to spell out the address of the flat to the officer. She never mentioned it.

An hour later both girls were sipping weak tea at the police station while they made their respective statements. It all seemed a pretty straightforward incident.

Carl had failed to turn up for an overtime shift that morning long before Sophie left London. Both girls explained the breakup and for the time being they were no longer needed in the investigation. The officer did make the comment that it was usual to find a note, but Sophie made no comment even though she noticed the subtle glance from Kelly.

As the comforting arms of her father folded around her and placed her gently in the passenger seat, Kelly offered to contact Niki for her and also to talk to John. They hugged, as her dad fastened the seatbelt she seemed incapable of dealing with. It felt wrong that she was being nursed and consoled as though she were the victim when she felt like the assailant. Perhaps the empathy was not meant to soften the blow of losing Carl but was in anticipation of the irreparable self-loathing that might dominate the rest of her life.

As she entered her parents' house, she expected the tearful open arms of her mum. Sophie knew she would have heard the door close and the kettle switched on by her dad, and yet she remained upstairs.

Sophie twizzled a cup of tea round and round without drinking any. It was obvious her mum blamed her even though her dad was trying to vindicate her. Mum had a soft spot for Carl so this would have hit her hard, but it was more than that. Dad had always been the more lenient parent while mum had made all the rules and made sure they were followed. The harsh reality at this moment was that she trusted her mother's judgment over dad's every time. Her mother had always been her moral compass and she knew long before she felt the sting of her mother's absence in the kitchen, that in this, she was definitely off-piste.

She watched the swirling liquid, warm and inviting with the aroma of home and wished she could stare at it forever or to melt through the seat on which she was sitting and disappear from this cruel world, and the unbearable sadness that drenched her aching heart.

She heard her mother's footsteps on the stairs and felt her enter the kitchen behind her. As she passed, she simply placed her hand on Sophie's shoulder. It was enough. It was more than she deserved, much more than she expected and she knew that it was as much as her mother could give right now.

Kelly's name lit up her phone.

"John will pick you up in the morning Sophie."

"Ok." Was all she could muster.

She ran a bath and sat in the warm water with her eyes tightly shut as though this might erase the entire day. Suddenly she let out a wail that seemed to come straight from her soul as the agony and grief finally found a voice.

Her mother rushed in and held her, rocking her in the frothy water as a mother tries to console a babe in arms. Her blouse soaking wet as she held her daughters head of dripping hair against her chest.

"Oh God Oh God Oh God!"

"It's ok Sophie. It will be ok."

Half an hour later, wrapped in a towel Sophie called Kelly.

"Why? Why? Why?" was all she could say "Why would he do that?"

There was silence for a few moments and then Kelly spoke softly.

"Don't you get it Sophie? You were his John."

Chapter 16

As daylight crept into the room, Sophie knew she had slept later than usual. She closed her eyes before assessing her surroundings. For the first time she was hoping to wake up in the world without John. The world where Carl was still happily in love with her after settling on white and crimson for their wedding flowers. Even if she awoke in her own vomit, on her dad's shed floor with the hangover from hell. The prospect of losing John had immeasurably diminished in comparison to this overwhelming remorse and horror. The knowledge that her loyal Carl had taken his own life rather than to live it without her.

Kelly's words had been like a knife through her heart. Carl couldn't live without her any more than she had been able to live without John and who was she to choose her own happiness over Carl's?

Today there was no need to check her surroundings, the clank of the teacup on her bedside table confirmed the continuation of her torture. Her heart sank.

What kind of a person was she? How could she have done this to him? She folded the pillow around her head as though trying to squeeze away the memories and images, hardly breathing through the dense pillow. Perhaps she could suffocate herself right there and disappear from all of this. A day ago, she had been happy and now she had been plummeted into the realms of despair and everyone would hate her again. As she lay in this isolation, breathing pillow scented air, she could feel the guilt starting to fade away and in its place a different feeling was beginning to grow. A feeling that was dissolving her remorse, absolving her of responsibility and nourishing her resolve to move forward. The feeling was anger. Her empathy for Carl was beginning to metamorphosize into pure anger.

This was Carl's fault not hers. His inability to get a grip on himself had spoiled everything and stolen her one chance at finally living a happy life with John. Now a dark cloud would hang over her tarnished future forever due to his selfishness. His pathetic inability to make a life for himself. Perhaps the driving force, as he climbed onto that damn chair was not the prospect of having to face life without her, but the satisfaction of imagining the utter destruction he knew he could wreak on her new life. Perhaps he believed that in taking his own life he would take hers with him.

She rushed to the bathroom to throw up again. She seemed to be doing nothing else of late, and that was his fault too. This would never blow over and no-one would ever forgive her, "Damn him!" she spat out the remaining lumps of vomit from her mouth, the acid burning her throat as she spat again and again, "damn him!"

She returned to the bedroom and got back into bed to take a sip of the warm tea hoping it would wash the acid taste from her mouth without triggering more retching. The room was a mess. Yesterday's crumpled clothes were strewn over the floor where she had stepped out of them without any ability to pick them up. The stench from them was making her nauseous. She tried to kick them away with the foot that was still dangling out of bed. She caught the edge of her trousers with her foot and as she tossed them, she noticed the slips of white paper protruding from a pocket.

Her heart sank. Tentatively she slid the two notes out of her pocket, placing the familiar note she had left for Carl on the bed whilst holding the other at arm's length as though it were an unexploded bomb.

He had written her name on the note in the perfect calligraphy he used for the cards and presents he gave her for Christmas and birthdays. She had bought him the set of pens when they first started dating and he had spent months practising. He had become quite an expert at producing beautifully scribed words with letters evenly sized and spaced, but her name on this particular slip of paper was a work of art. He had taken his time over her name, forming each letter to perfection with the flourishes flicked out at the start and finish of each one.

Her hand was shaking as she tried to decide if or not, she wanted to hear Carl's last words. She closed her eyes tightly, unfolded the note, took a deep breath and then opened them. The note was blank, totally blank. At first, she thought she had it the wrong way round and flipped it over and back before realisation delivered the blow. Carl had absolutely nothing to say to her. It felt worse than any explanation he could give, worse than any unleashed anger or venomous insult. It was the biggest insult he could give. He had nothing to say to her. She was nothing. He was nothing and there was nothing left.

She put the notes in the back of her purse without knowing why she wanted to keep them, and started to prepare herself for John's arrival and her return to London. Today there was no titivating, no urgent need to make herself attractive. The knot in the pit of her stomach, the ache in her chest, the sick feeling in her throat were blocking any feeling of anticipation or any hint of pleasure. She looked at herself in the mirror and embraced the fact that she was a mess, without wanting to do anything about it. The outside matched the ugliness within, and it seemed appropriate to leave it that way. She slid back under the sheets noticing the rancid odour of her unwashed body and curled up in acceptance of her own repulsion.

John arrived later the same day and had a whispered conversation downstairs as though she were child, but she didn't care. She had neither the strength nor the will to object and instead, chose to withdraw inside an imaginary wall that would be her protection for the next few days while she tried to organise and control her emotions.

She descended the stairs to the distant chatter of inquests, funerals and the devastation of his parents which her mum repeatedly stated would be unbearable. Everyone seemed intent on stating the obvious to add further weight to her existing burden. She had no capacity to hear any of it, to consider any of it or to feel any of it, her head was already bursting. There was no room in her brain for anything more, her brain was already occupied with nothing at all, it was like her entire thought process had been totally blocked.

John put his arm around her as he offered her a bowl of soup with his other hand. She shook her head gently.

"Darling you need to eat."

She looked up at him through sunken dark-circled eyes.

"What have I done John?"

"Don't Soph," he squeezed her gently, "you can't blame yourself for this. You can't stay with someone who loves you if you don't love them back."

"Why not?"

"What do you mean why not?"

"If someone loves you and wants you so badly then how can staying be such a bad thing?"

John didn't answer. This was no time to argue his point, so he just brushed her unwashed hair from her blotchy face and kissed her hand.

She sighed deeply, almost desperately.

"Things will get better when we go home darling."

"Home?" The word warmed her with a little hope for a moment.

"Back to London, but first you need to decide what you want to do up here."

"I know" she sighed again. "what do you think I should do?"

"I think it depends on his parents and how they feel. I know you want to stay for the funeral, but I also know you want to run away from this. You need to do what feels respectful. Perhaps the best thing you could do to help would be to leave."

Sophie looked shocked. This was about Carl, her Carl and his family, her family. It felt beyond reason that she was the person who would be excluded from everything. They were meant to be married and now she had less right to be near him than a complete stranger.

"Do you want me to find out how they feel?" The voice came from the kitchen door and without looking up Sophie knew Niki had returned to her life.

Niki walked over to Sophie pushing John firmly aside.

"Now come on, get up those stairs and get washed, you look a fright. Then get dressed and I'll go and find out how the land lies. Once you know where you need to be, we can work out how to get you through these next few weeks."

"Weeks?" Sophie frowned.

"This isn't going to be over any time soon," Niki said softly, "inquests can take months and it may be weeks before they even release him for a funeral."

" I.. I can't do this."

"Yes, you can" Niki pushed her bodily towards the door, "off you go. Shower, hair, makeup and dressed please."

As Sophie obeyed, her mum smiled gratefully, and John nodded his approval.

As soon as she thought Sophie was out of earshot, Niki spoke directly to John for the first time.

"How are you bearing up?"

"It's hard. I can't pretend that I'm not to blame for this can I?"

His sincerity sounded warm and Sophie saw Niki hug him through the slightly open door as though he were a lifelong friend.

"It's not your fault."

John looked up through his unkempt hair and raised his eyebrows in contradiction.

"I'm going to find out if she will be welcome at the funeral," Niki continued, "you take care of her and I'll be in touch."

Niki left without saying goodbye to Sophie, leaving John to try to hold them all together. He'd arranged two days off work, but Sophie didn't ask him about it. She had lost track of the days and was still having difficulty holding any food inside her body. She didn't notice the hours passing nor the way John was mooching around without purpose, her mind was frozen, and her only thoughts were questions and replays or horrific images.

She slept that night with John in her childhood bed with her back towards him. He didn't try to touch or console her in any way and she was content with that. She thought it unlikely that she would ever want to be touched by anyone again.

The next morning after her usual throwing up of the tea she had just swallowed, she lay on the bed beside John and put her hand in his. He squeezed it gently and she wanted to talk to him, but her mind was as empty as Carl's note. There was nothing useful to say.

As day turned back to night, she lay silently in the darkness beside John wishing she could tell him everything. Then at least he might understand a lot better than he did at that moment. A few weeks ago, she and Carl had been relatively happy and yet both of them had been driven to suicide because of her infatuation with John. She sighed again, sighing and vomiting seemed to take up most of her waking hours.

She turned to look at John in the small glimmer of light afforded by the outside streetlamp and he glanced back at her a little uncomfortably. His confident personality and cheeky sense of humour had evaporated. Swallowed up in this sobering tragedy until he too now lay silently, frozen in the same void as everyone else around her.

"I'm sorry." was all she could say.

"For what?"

"For dragging you into this misery."

"I don't remember being dragged anywhere." A glimmer of a smile touched the edges of his mouth.

She smiled back more from affection than humour.

"How can you still love me? I'm a mess. Why are you even still here?"

He smiled more confidently because they were finally talking again.

"Well, I admit that you are all vomit and skin and bone," he squeezed her skinny arm demonstratively, "skin and bone."

She frowned at her arm as his large hand almost circled it fully.

"Oh God. I'm disgusting?"

He let go of her arm and put his own huge arm around her body pulling her close.

"Do you know how I know that I love you?"

She shook her head.

"Because there is nothing at all I could ever find distasteful about you, no matter what."

"Really? I feel exactly the same." She allowed herself to see this glimmer of hope.

"I felt it from the moment we met." His voice was so sincere she felt the goose bumps she had so desperately missed.

"Me too." She whispered.

He kissed her forehead, and for the first time since she had left him behind in London, she felt sure of something again.

The following day John had to return to London.

"I was meant to be back at work today love, but if I set off now, I'll make it for mid-morning." he whispered before jumping out of bed and padding off to the bathroom.

Sophie was sitting up by the time he returned.

"Is it Monday?" she asked.

"Yep" he replied, "do you want me to make you some tea and toast before I leave?"

"I'll get some myself after you've gone."

"You won't though, will you? Sophie, you have to start eating. There's no wonder you keep throwing up, your stomach has forgotten what food is for. I'll make some in a minute, but you need to see a doctor about getting your appetite back before it turns to anorexia!"

She knew he was right. Her stomach felt incapable of retaining even a morsel of food and as she stared at the toast, she wished he would hurry up and leave so she didn't have to force it down.

"Come on. Try a bit."

She took a sip of tea and tore off a lump of toast which she chewed energetically to appease him and then audibly swallowed.

"Good girl."

She took another bite and washed it down with more tea.

He walked to the door and picked up his case but before he could get through it, she ran by him, knocking him out of the way on her dash to the toilet.

"Doctor!" he called to her through the half-open door.

"Ok." She gasped between retching.

Later that day she sat in the surgery while a new young doctor took her blood pressure and heart rate, even though she had told him categorically that she was suffering from shock and needed something to calm her.

He looked her up and down for a few moments

"Any other symptoms?"

"Sometimes I feel dizzy, but I think that's because I can't seem to hold any food down."

"Could you be pregnant?"

She tipped her head to one side curiously.

"Pregnant? I'm suffering from shock and grief and guilt and despair not pregnancy."

He smiled condescendingly. "Let's do a test to be sure."

"Ok ok" She said irritably but as she handed him the sample she was quickly trying to remember if this could be possible.

She couldn't remember who she had made love to when or if she had been remembering to take her pill, in all the chaos between reality and dreams.

"Aha!" He said triumphantly

"I'm not.......?"

"Yes, you are," he smiled "that explains the sickness. Perhaps this will give you something positive to focus on?"

"I don't know." Her head was spinning as she tried to calculate ovulation from her last period. She couldn't think here. She needed to find her diary. She needed this idiot to stop smiling at her like it was good news.

"I need to go."

"But there are some things I need to talk to you about."

"Not right now. I'll make another appointment." She left the door open on her way out and later would not be able to recall any part the journey back from the doctor to her parent's house.

She checked the pages of her dairy over and over. Last period, ovulation, sex, but the answer was the same. She was pregnant with Carl's baby.

Chapter 17

Back in the privacy of the bathroom, she tried to get her thoughts into some sort of logical order so she could decide who she should tell about this. If anyone.

She was sure John had said his family were catholic, which meant abortion would be off the table if he shared their beliefs. The honest thing to do, the decent and moral thing to do would be to share her dilemma with John so they could decide together but it seemed pointless. If he wanted her to get an abortion, then they would probably both share the guilt of it and if he wanted her to keep it, they would be starting a new life together with another man's child. She imagined placing that child in John's arms and tried to imagine how it would feel. A father looking down at the miracle he didn't make. The tiny face of Carl's child resting in the place his own child should have been.

Either way, none of this would be the perfect life she dreamed of, and she swiftly concluded that sometimes, in the pursuit of perfection, sacrifices have to be made.

She would tell no-one.

"Sophie?" her mother was knocking gently on the bathroom door, "you have a letter, and it looks official"

"How did it get to your house?"

"I think you gave my address to the Police, didn't you? I had to sign for it."

"Open it mum, what is it?"

"You have an appointment to make a formal statement at the Police station."

"Why?"

"It will be all about establishing his state of mind I should think. They'll be collecting facts for the inquest."

Sophie opened the door.

"I can't do it."

"Yes, you can. With no note or last words to anyone, of course they are going to have to get statements from everyone. That's unusual for a suicide."

She noticed a marked difference in her mother, who was biting her bottom lip with tension. She seemed to have aged ten years in five days. Her once laughing eyes hung limply at the corners emphasising dark bags and her cheeks sagged giving her mouth a downturned expression. It looked like she had done nothing to her hair for several days which was now greasy and flat in patches where she had slept on it.

Suddenly remembering the image of her mum's head stained with blood from the operation turned her cold. It all seemed so vivid, not like a dream at all but like another time, a time she remembered well. She had not worried about her own mental illness for some time and quickly shook the image from her head.

"Suppose so."

In her mind she replaced the word inquest with trial. This was to be 'the trial of Sophie.' No-one would say it, but everyone knew it. The coroner may well record a verdict of suicide, but the verdict of murder would be on the faces of every one of Carls family and friends.

The noble thing to do would be to submit Carl's note and accept the blame but there seemed to be no point in fanning the flames of hatred which were already out of control. Perhaps it was fitting to regard it as a trial because there were so many victims and with so many victims how could there not have been a crime? There was a time when 'breach of promise' used to be a crime and today she understood why, because a broken heart is every bit as brutal and damaging as physical assault or even murder.

Self-loathing and vindication tipped the scales of justice in her mind back and forth with equal momentum and rhythm day after day. She was grateful that John didn't have to witness this pendulum personality and with him safely out of the way she could vent her desperation without worrying about losing his respect or admiration. Without risking the loss of his love.

"Let me know when the funeral is, and I will come back for it and then we can go back home together." He suggested on their regular evening call.

She felt annoyed that he would even suggest showing up at the funeral, but she hid her disappointment for his lack of sensitivity

"It would look better if you were not there, love. I don't want to rub everyone's nose in it." She was trying to be subtle.

"I would be there for you, not everyone else." He protested.

She became even more annoyed that he wasn't getting it.

"It's not about me though is it? Or you? The funeral is for Carl. I want to be there for him and that means that you can't be there for me!" She suspected he just wanted to prove she belonged to him now, maybe even to flaunt that she had chosen him over Carl.

It was the first time she had displayed any negativity towards him, and he sounded wounded by it.

"I'm sorry, I suppose I wasn't thinking."

She looked down at her phone as though trying to determine if he was being a supportive partner or an egotistical ass hole.

"No, I don't think you were." It was a neutral, non-judgemental response.

"Well, I'm sorry, and yes of course you must go alone. This is about you and Carl, not me."

"Thank you." She said softly

"Look I need to go," he said abruptly, "I'll call tomorrow."

He ended the call, and she knew she had hurt his feelings. She felt frustrated with herself and with him.

Was she now choosing Carl over John? Carl was gone and if she didn't watch herself, she might end up with no-one, with nothing.

She would call him later and try to repair the damage but for now she was still annoyed that he thought it appropriate to turn up at the funeral, adding insult to grief for Carl's family and more poignantly, to be holding her hand in the presence of Carl's dead body. Still, she would apologise later.

The next two weeks consisted of days full of nothing other than the routine of physical existence and the exhaustion of constantly treading water. Empty hours punctuated by the emerging and fading of memories and visions. She was breathing in and out, putting food in her mouth occasionally and waiting.

Waiting for the funeral date to be set, waiting for the conversations to evolve into something other than Carl's tragic death, waiting for herself to heal, waiting for some spark of joy to return. In the meantime, she could do nothing other than be absorbed in the many elements of the mess that had become her life.

She hoped that at some point in the near future, the inquest would afford her some degree of closure, release her from this static existence back to her new home, but she couldn't imagine ever feeling good, content or joyous ever again.

Drowning in the well-meant clichés lavished on her, she refused to take refuge in any of them. Time is definitely not a healer, suicide victims are not inherently unbalanced to start with, all is definitely not fair in love and war and as for love conquering all, well her love had conquered and annihilated her entire life.

Amid her grief there was also the torment of the biggest secret of all, growing silently inside her, adding unbearable weight to her already intolerable burden.

She wanted to tell her mum about her pregnancy but couldn't possibly inflict any more worry on the poor woman. She hated keeping the secret from John but the physical distance between them together with her emotional isolation had taken its toll.

She knew the love between them was still strong and soon she would be able to put the effort into rebuilding it to its former glory, but now was not the time to reveal something like this.

If he had been by her side, if they were able to hold each other and see each other's eyes, she might have had the confidence to share her problem but right now, she was not going to risk pushing their relationship to the point of no return.

She told herself that they would have the conversation when she returned to London, they would make the decision together, but her stomach turned over whenever she imagined that conversation. It was a huge risk and a risk she didn't want to take, not now and not ever. So, in a fleeting moment of insecurity, the decision was made, the phone was already in her hand and the fate of another soul had been sealed. She had to arrange an abortion as soon as possible.

She laid the phone back down on her bed and propped herself against the pillows with her hands resting unwittingly on her stomach. As soon as she realised, she moved them away and folded them across her chest. She couldn't bear for her child to feel comforted by the touch of its mother's hands. Hands that promised the instinctive maternal protection that should have been its unequivocal right. This child was not so lucky. There was something stronger than a mother's instinct at play and it was nothing more than the need to preserve the love of the man craved.

In the days between decision and appointment Sophie was haunted in so many ways. She remembered the words of the clairvoyant who had told her she would have a son with Carl. She wondered if an aborted child fulfilled the premonition adequately. She had also been having terrible dreams or maybe they were just guilt infused delusions.

Twice she thought she had heard Carl's voice. It was in the semiconscious state between sleep and waking that she heard him say her name. He was calling her as though he were trying to get her attention. She tried to convince herself that it was a perfectly normal reaction to the stress of what she was trying to deal with, but it was enough to make her cancel her appointment. She needed more time to think. Her conscience had finally found a voice and repeatedly hearing Carl's was more than a little unsettling.

On the second occasion John had rung her while she was still in the grip of terror

"Are you alright, you sound terrible?"

"I .. I'm not sure. Do you believe in ghosts?"

"Definitely not" John laughed "Why?"

"I keep hearing Carl's voice."

"I'm not bloody surprised! So do I, and I never met the bloke."

He had said enough to calm her down. He had also said enough to make her realise how much she still loved him and his inappropriate but unoffensive humour.

"Do you want me to come back up there?"

"No. No. I'm just being an idiot. Forget I said it."

"Is there a date for the funeral yet?"

"Not exactly but we heard they had given permission to release the body."

Hearing herself refer to Carl as 'the body' felt sickening.

"Sophie?" John was worried by the long silence that she hadn't even noticed she'd created.

"Yes, sorry. I was just thinking that I probably don't have anything suitable in black to wear." She lied.

Clothes were the last thing on her mind. The only thought was that Carl, the man who made stir fry on Tuesdays was now just a body.

"I don't think anyone will be noticing what you're wearing." John continued oblivious to what was really going on.

She tried to get back into the conversation but the fact that she had been responsible for turning her gorgeous Carl into a body on a mortuary slab was a difficult fact to ignore.

"No, I don't suppose anyone will care what I wear." She concurred.

Even so, she was already looking through her clothes with the phone to her ear. She pulled a black suit out of the wardrobe and held it up to the light.

There it was, the stain she had failed to get out since the day Carl dabbed her with engine grease when he proposed. He had picked her up and spun her around when she said yes, and the forlorn grease mark bore witness to his joy. She fondled the stain affectionately, remembering Carl's arms around her, the smell of car engines mixed with his stale aftershave. The sickly yet wonderful stench of nostalgia.

"Are you still there?" John's voice was distant on the handset.

"Yes. I'm here." She said almost too cheerily

"How are you feeling?"

"Just want to get it over with." She lied while wondering what had just happened and why she was suddenly missing Carl.

She rushed John off of the phone. Something she had never ever wanted to do before, but she was caught up in a moment she couldn't share with him and needed to try something.

"Carl?"

She listened for his reply

"Carl? Are you here?"

There was no reply, but it didn't stop her from having the conversation with him. She gently stroked her belly and imagined the tiny child sleeping innocently inside her. A tiny miracle she had made with Carl. The man who loved her more than anyone ever had and who would have been the most adoring father imaginable.

"If you can hear me, I want to tell you that I'm sorry. I have made this… this big mess of everything and you didn't deserve any of it. And now we are having a baby. Yes, you and I made a baby, can you believe that? I don't know what to do Carl, I don't know what to do and I am missing you even though I tell myself that I'm not"

She slid to her knees.

"Who are you talking to?" her mother was standing over her, "are you praying?"

"Something like that."

She held her arms up to her mother in the way a baby plea's to be picked up and her mother instinctively reached out, pulling her up to her feet and holding her close. No words were spoken. Everything was understood without the words, just like Carl's note.

As the days slid by, she got into a strangely comforting routine living at her parents. With no job to go to and no point in returning to London until after the funeral she seemed to have awarded herself permission to squander the time while nursing her grief.

She would get up halfway through the morning and eat breakfast in her pyjamas. She would shower and go shopping with her mum, drink coffee in the local tearoom she used to be taken into as a child for a special treat, and then return home and help to cook tea for the three of them.

There was something wholesome about the routine and at times she almost resented the interruptions from John. It wasn't that she loved him any less, but he was an abrupt reminder that she had bigger issues to consider other than which soap opera to watch with mum and dad. This small world filled with small decisions and no confrontations became her safe haven and she found herself wondering why people ever complicate their lives at all.

As she sat looking out into the back garden at the same view she had seen as a child, she visualised herself with Kelly on the garden swing singing rhymes about the men they would marry when they grew up.

She wiped away a salty tear which was tickling the side of her nose and recalled the girly sleepovers of early teens and giggles over boys and plans of living happily in the same street when they married. She wiped again and recalled her Friday night feeling of meeting up in the local pub for a meal and a drink to start the weekend, she was wiping more quickly as the tears fell more readily making her face wet and sore as her throat closed in dry gulping sobs.

She quickly tried to compose herself at hearing Niki's voice in the kitchen and then the door opened, and Niki barged in.

"Have you been crying? Niki's tone was almost reprimanding.

"Maybe a little."

Niki's tone softened.

"Sophie, I needed to tell you something in person before you hear it"

"What is it?"

"It was Carl's funeral yesterday."

Sophie hardly reacted at all.

"So that's it then? He's gone now?"

"Are you ok about it?"

"Yes. I didn't really expect to be invited. Did you go?"

"Yes. I thought you might hate me for not telling you about it, but they didn't want you turning up"

Sophie looked at her friend with an expression that showed the depth of the pain she was in and how nothing so trivial could really hurt her now.

"I don't hate you" She walked over and gave Niki a hug "I'm glad you were there for him"

"Kelly didn't go. She said it would be betraying you and that you had as much right as anyone to pay your respects to him."

Sophie shook her head and smiled. Who would have thought that little air head Kelly would turn out to be so full of loyalty? She wanted to ask about the funeral, who spoke, what was said but she was too afraid of what she might hear, so instead she settled on polite interest.

"Did it go alright? Well as much as these things can?"

Niki didn't answer.

"Nik?"

Niki kept her eyes to the floor.

"What?"

Eventually, reluctantly Niki raised her swollen eyes.

"It wasn't great Soph."

Sophie cocked her head questioningly.

"Sophie it was awful." She couldn't hold back the emotion.

"What do you mean?" Sophie was asking a question she didn't want to know the answer to.

"I can't describe it. Just so much sobbing, so much heartbreak and his mum ... oh God his mum" Niki held onto the wall for support as she broke down.

Sophie wanted to hold Niki and comfort her, but she didn't feel entitled to. She was the perpetrator, the evil reason for all this pain. Instead, she just covered her face with her hands as though hiding from the spectacle in front of her.

For several minutes no-one spoke, no-one moved, gentle sobs and shallow breathing were the only indication that anyone was in the room at all.

In the distance Sophie could hear children playing. Distant laughter, carefree infants having fun in the spring sunshine. Squeals of joy piercing their misery with its cruel irony. If it hadn't been for the need to drown out the happy sounds Sophie may have allowed the limbo to continue but it became unbearable and eventually, she was the first to speak.

"I am so sorry." Was all she could say.

"I know." Niki's tone felt cold and harsh.

"If I could go back and change it Niki I would."

"Would you?" The question was accusing, condemning.

Sophie knew it was her cue to weep and to beat her chest in self-loathing but there was little point. Her sentence had already been passed and it was a fair judgment, so instead, she returned to the silence and the distant happy chorus of children at play.

She sat down on the sofa and looked out through the window longing to be anywhere other than where she was right now. Wishing this moment would end and she could be spared the contempt and hatred of what had very recently been her dearest friend.

Her eyes still fixed firmly on some point in the distance and her ears on the children at play she heard the door close as her wish was granted. It was the last time the two friends would speak.

Chapter18

The following morning, she was still in her room, looking out of the window at the same view. She noticed the flowers were starting to bloom. New life springing up all around and right here in her own body was another new life, full of hope and expectation yet its fate was yet undetermined. The anguish of the decision had taken over from the many other anxieties which had consumed her from the start of this turbulent year.

She longed for just one person to talk to about it, but she had already decided to deny herself that luxury. Sharing a secret of this magnitude would only lead to a lifetime of worry and she didn't want to put herself in the position of being beholden to anyone. She needed total control.

She had only two options and whichever she chose, it would be hers alone, and if she chose to abort, she would not create any danger that someone might one day blurt it out in anger or drunkenness, destroying her life all over again.

She could have the termination without telling a soul or she could tell John the truth and keep the baby in the hope he would want to bring it up as his own. She was fairly sure he would, but she also knew it would in some way, taint the perfect life she had imagined for them. Was it a risk she was willing to take? She needed to speak to John.

"Morning are you on your way to work?"

"Sure am. Reception's not good on the train. We might get cut off. Do you need something?" he sounded concerned.

She hated the way he automatically assumed she had another problem for him to deal with.

"No. I just wanted to hear your voice."

"That's nice. When are you coming back?"

"The minute the funeral is over." She lied. She needed more time up north.

"Can't wait."

She took a deep breath. She needed to sound him out.

"Me neither. Now we can go full steam ahead and start to build a new future."

"Well let's hope nothing else bites us in the arse eh?"

She pretended to laugh. "Like what?"

"I don't know I was just kidding. We do seem to get more than our fair share of problems though, don't we?"

"Suppose we do but we've managed so far."

"Yes, we have. Thank God it's all behind us. I don't think I could take any more chaos."

She'd heard enough. She couldn't hand him another disaster.

"Have a good day at work and I'll see you soon then."

"Ok Love."

She ended the call and sat for a moment with her head in her hands.

She pretended that she was not taking the decision lightly, lying to herself about considering both options but the verdict was already in. Was the life of her unborn child worth more to her than a picture-perfect life with John? No, it wasn't. The death sentence was passed for a second time, in a cold and calculated heartbeat.

She rang the clinic again and made another appointment for the next day. She needed to get this over with quickly. Not for fear of changing her mind, but because now that the fate of this tiny life had been sealed, the guilt of continuing to nourish it felt unbearably cruel and deceitful. As deceitful and cold as the heart of a sheep farmer, lovingly cradling his bottle-fed lambs when the slaughterhouse is already booked.

She needed to relieve her heart of the burden as quickly as possible. The sickening self-loathing she felt for her own soul, as she repeatedly rejected pleas for a reprieve for her unborn child. The mother inside her was no match for the single-minded woman who now had the perfect life finally within her grasp. Her chance at real happiness was about to commence and nothing was going to stand in the way. She was about to sweep this from her life in the same ruthless way she had swept away Carl and everything else that had stood in her path.

All she had to do was to get through the next twenty-four hours and promise herself she would never utter a word of this to a living soul.

The afternoon seemed endless, but she was thankful that darkness still fell early at this time of year and her mum didn't question her when she took to her bed before nine o'clock.

"Is there anything I can get you darling?" Her mother was stroking her hair the way she had when she'd had the chicken pox.

"A cup of tea would be nice."

The crow's feet spread from the corners of those weathered eyes like rays of sunshine from behind a cloud, warming Sophie's frozen heart and causing her to feel entitled to her mother's unconditional love. Though her love for John was overpowering, passionate and fervid there was no comparison to this gentle selfless love of a mother for her child. The irony of it failed to infiltrate her mind, failed to arouse her own maternal instinct and failed to hinder her ruthless plan. For a moment she simply embraced the good fortune she had been blessed with and the protection it afforded.

But as she smiled back, with her hand resting on her belly, dread was rising up inside her again, challenging her decision again. Mother nature's bond between mother and child was testing her resolve. She knew she had to fight it and not allow this moment of sentiment to alter the course of her life. As she snatched her hand away and slammed it down beside her, she silently accepted that the love she had once craved and described as 'a love to die for' it seemed, was also 'a love to kill for.'

"Half a sugar please." She abruptly interrupted her own thought.

As she waited for the tea to arrive her phone was flashing on the bedside table. She had forgotten it was on silent and picked it up noticing six missed calls from John.

"Shit." She reprimanded herself out loud.

She had been so preoccupied with managing her secrets she had totally forgotten about the reason behind it all. She quickly dialled his number.

"Thank God." Was John's opening line.

"I know. I'm sorry. It's been mad, this afternoon."

"So?"

She had so much going on for a moment she couldn't think what he meant.

"So what?"

"The funeral? Any news?"

After tomorrow there was no reason to delay her return, so she decided to tell him.

"I missed it." She didn't feel like elaborating.

"What? How could you have missed it?"

"I only found out an hour ago," she lied "it's a long story but it seems no-one wanted me there so no-one told me it was happening."

There was a long silence.

"John?"

"Yes, I'm still here."

"Why aren't you saying anything?"

"Well, I can't really say I'm surprised. I mean, if it were my son then I'm sure........"

"You're sure you wouldn't want the bitch who killed him there! Well, you have blood on your hands too you know!" It was vicious and unfair, but she was tired of wearing the murderer badge alone

"Sophie. You're understandably upset but it was right that you weren't there."

"I know," her tone had mellowed from exhaustion, "I'll pack up and come back on Friday."

"But it's only Wednesday." He said sulkily.

"I know but I've got a few loose ends to tie up." She needed to give herself at least one day after the abortion before making the journey.

"Ok, but you better ring me every day. I was worried and anyway I'm bloody missing you."

She grinned from ear to ear.

"That's the best news I've heard for ages."

"Well you better believe it and make sure you get rid of all your loose ends for good, because we don't want them following us around."

She blew him several noisy kisses before taking the cup of tea from her mum.

"Was that John?"

"Yes."

"You two still ok?"

"Couldn't be better." She sipped the tea trying to ignore the loose end that she might never be able to tie up no matter how effectively she managed to keep her hands away from her belly. She was pretty sure it might follow her around in the way John had described, but at least she could carry that haunting alone and protect John from feeling the guilt and shame of it. By tomorrow it would be gone. Another death to add to her murderous baggage.

The inquest was also looming and this time she would have to attend and face his family. To walk among their despair and grief knowing that she had been the cause of it.

"Night love." The door clicked shut and she was alone with her thoughts.

She tried to focus on her new life, on nights out with John in the city, entertaining his friends and business colleagues, buying a house with a garden somewhere in the suburbs , raising a family and just being blissfully happy with her soul-mate right beside her. This was her destiny. This was the life she always dreamt of and all she had to do was to endure the clinic visit tomorrow and the inquest. Then it was all hers for the taking.

She could hardly hold her eyes open although her tea was still beside her. She picked it up again and took a few more sips with her head propped on the pillow, allowing herself to cradle the warm cup and doze for a moment. The living sounds of clanking pots and cupboard doors beneath her, were becoming more distant as her eyes closed and the tension melted from her face. She was feeling so relaxed that the gentle kiss on her lips was received as gently as it was placed.

"I miss you." Carl's voice was too familiar to startle her.

"We are going to have a baby," he whispered softly "Isn't that amazing?"

She shot up in her bed and scanned the room in terror.

"Who is this?"

She was speaking out loud to an empty and silent room.

"Where are you?"

Her screams were drowned out by the banging of footsteps on the stairs.

"Sophie?" Her dad's hand was suddenly on her forehead, "what is it?"

Her eyes wide with terror, she scanned the room back and forth.

"I don't know."

"Did you have a nightmare?"

"I don't know."

"Do you want me to stay here for a while? Shall I get your mum?"

"I don't know."

She didn't know anything. Nothing except that her dad's rough hand in hers felt like a lifeline and she was gripping it harder than was comfortable for either of them.

"I thought I......." She didn't finish.

"What Sophie? You thought what?"

Caution stepped in before she said any more. She suspected she'd had a hallucination caused by the guilt she was feeling about her plan to kill Carl's baby. Her dad mustn't know anything of this.

"Nothing dad. Just a nightmare."

She released the grip on his hand, for which he seemed relieved and made an attempt to smile.

He ran his hand through his imaginary hair which had deserted him a decade earlier, and then held her hand more loosely.

"I'm ok now."

"You sure?"

She nodded confidently but after he left, she picked up one of her mother's books to distract her and tried to absorb the words. It was something about the British land army women of world war two. The hardships and relationships with American soldiers and the secrets they tried to keep, the pregnancies they tried to hide. It all felt too close to home right now and she wished she could just fast forward to Friday. As she skipped through the pages as though trying to find the solution to her own dilemma, she imagined herself on Friday morning, when all her baggage could be left behind as she packed up her car and headed off for her new life with John.

The heroine in the book was having no such luck as she wrestled with her conscience and decided to struggle through life in the hope that her British husband would return from war and just accept her American bastard. She threw the book down in frustration at the fictitious woman's stupidity in throwing her happiness away for the sake of a bit of unwanted baggage. She looked down at her belly, the problem would be gone soon, and she just knew that on Friday she would feel like the school exams were over and the long summer holiday was stretching out before her.

She picked up a magazine and pen instead and turned to the crossword until sheer exhaustion dropped her blissfully into the depths of uninterrupted sleep.

Chapter 19

Early on Friday morning Sophie Taylor packed up her little car with just about everything she owned and was on her way south to join the M1 and start her new life. She was hoping to reach the first services before she bled through her clothes once again.

She had not expected the bleeding to be this heavy nor for the cramps to continue so strongly. She had no plan on how she was going to handle this with John other than to tell him she was having a very heavy period. She wanted everything to be so perfect and this predicament was a million miles away from her image of a romantic start to a happy future.

In the last two days, the practicality of dealing with these blood-soaked sanitary towels had caused her much more concern and distress than the loss of the son or daughter she had just ripped from her body and discarded. Any sentiment had been tossed aside with the book about the stupid land army woman who thought it a good idea to carry an accidental baby of a man who was no longer around, allowing it to destroy any chance of happiness with her husband. The book lay on the bedroom floor, angrily rejected and soon to be forgotten just like the fleeting moment of empathy she'd had for her sleeping baby.

It was a long journey in which she wriggled and fidgeted through every mile, popping pain killers and repeatedly hoping she would make it to the next service station before she bled onto the seat.

She had been warned not to use tampons or to have intercourse for fear of infection but had already decided to take the risk of swapping towels for tampons at the last services.

She bought several boxes of super-plus and tied two together hoping that inserted in tandem they might stem the flow. As she looked at her watch, she was thankful she hadn't told John the time she had left Filey. Each visit to a service station was taking almost half an hour by the time she had parked the car, walked into the place, sometimes queued for the toilet and got back on the road. The journey which should have taken about four hours had taken six already.

As she finally pulled up outside his apartment building, she hoped he would not make a big deal of welcoming her return. She wanted to slip quietly into the shower, wrap herself in a towel and get into bed alone. The only way to make that happen was to fake a migraine and as she opened the car door and took out one small case, she caught a glimpse of her reflection. She already looked like a woman with a migraine.

As the lift door opened her heart sank. She could already hear music playing from his flat and knew he must have been watching for her arrival through the window.

As the familiar bouncy melody of "Two can have a party" infiltrated the lobby she took a deep breath. The lift door had closed, and it was already on its decent of abandonment. There was nowhere to go other than forward into the façade behind that door and as she stood pondering her options, it flew open to reveal a chubby man in a party hat grinning with a fruit filled cocktail in his hand.

Before she could perfect her migraine face, he pulled her into the room and spun her around. On the table were two plates on which he had lovingly halved a selection of party food and in the centre stood a huge cake covered in doves and the boldly iced words "Will You Marry Me?"

Sophie closed her eyes and sighed. She hoped her despair would be interpreted as something else. This was the moment. The one she would be asked about time and again. The moment she would one day share with their children.

She buried her head in his chest allowing the tears to fall but desperately fighting to contain the sobs pushing to be released. He seemed content with her reaction and as he lovingly peeled a strand of hair from her wet cheek and kissed her forehead. She could feel that for him, the moment was perfect, it was exactly how he had imagined and as she winced under another surge of stomach cramp and felt the trickle of blood making its way down her thigh, she couldn't imagine a worse moment than this.

"I'll take that as a yes," he smiled, "come on, dry your eyes, our party starts right here, and it will last until one of us croaks."

She raised her eyebrows and tried to be more receptive.

"I feel like I have arrived at a party at eleven o'clock when everyone else is already drunk."

As he spun her around again, she could feel the droplet accelerate down her inner thigh.

"Then you have some catching up to do."

"Sure do," she smiled as she gulped the cocktail, "I'll just nip to the toilet. Been dying to go for the last fifty miles."

As she left the room she gently and quietly picked up her bag and marched into the bathroom.

In the toilet she removed the soaking tampons and sat for a few moments listening to the steady drip of blood hitting the water below. She knew if she took too long, he'd be knocking on the door, so she quickly opened two more tampons and tied the strings together. She then wet some toilet roll and attempted to clean herself up with the soggy paper and bathroom soap. She added a backup wad of folded paper to her underwear before pulling a pair of jeans out of her case and pulling them on to hold everything firmly in place. Her skirt was rammed harshly into the case and within a moment she returned to the hallway and threw open the door to join the party.

"What happened to your skirt?" He mused, blatantly disinterested in his own question.

"Had a ladder." She lied.

He made no comment and as they danced, he chatted excitedly about all the plans he was making but her heart was aching. This was the night she had been proposed to and it was not how things were supposed to be. It was supposed to be perfect the way it is for everyone else but then she wondered if it's all just an illusion. Did all those happy brides she had envied hold some deep secret or regret in their heart? That one thing that spoiled their perfect day?

One of her very first memories as an infant had been sitting on her mum's knee to wait for Princess Diana to walk down the aisle in her beautiful dress. The memory followed her into her envious teens yet, the years uncovered the reality of that day and how the pain in those eyes had been cleverly hidden from the entire nation. Was true love a total myth? The second-best kept secret to Santa Clause? She couldn't answer the questions her bruised heart was asking, partly because they challenged her fairy tale dream and partly because the cocktails were being consumed at a faster rate than her body could handle.

Whatever the answers were, this would always be the day in which the love of her life had thrown her a private party and proposed. The moment he had placed a diamond ring on her finger on the balcony overlooking the city lights while the remnants of Carl's baby soaked through her jeans.

She tried to sober up with several glasses of water as John sat drunkenly in his laziboy chair, which gave her the opportunity to drop in the fact that she was having a heavy period and excuse herself to take a shower.

"It doesn't have to stop us from making love" he protested as she emerged feeling cleaner but non the less vulnerable "this is a special night."

Sophie knew he would say that.

"Really John I can't tonight. There will be lots and lots of nights for love making."

She sat gingerly on the bed as she watched him hopping around drunkenly trying to pull his leg out of his trousers. Still hopping with one leg bent upwards, captured by the material in his fist, he looked up and grinned.

"Come here."

She was getting a bit irritated, but she could tell from his face that this was not going to go away without making the night an even worse memory.

"How about..." she said teasingly as she dropped to her knees and unzipped him.

He smiled but his disappointment couldn't be hidden.

"I don't want you to do me a favour." He said taking her wrists and pulling her back to her feet.

"I want to share this moment with you. Inside you."

She looked at him sympathetically. Suddenly he grinned.

"We could make love in the shower." He said picking her up and carrying her in.

"Ok ok, but let me get undressed first."

She left him trying to remove the remainder of his clothes while she returned to the toilet to remove the tandem tampons. She sat for a while until she could hear the water running and then made a quick dash for the shower cubicle using her hand to catch any drips of blood on the way. As she pulled back the screen, she put her hand behind him into the spray as she kissed him passionately in order to hold his attention above ground level and at first things didn't feel too bad.

She soaped him down and he was instantly aroused by her slippery hands sliding over his body, teasing and provoking the erection which was now pressing against her stomach despite the alcohol he'd consumed. He pulled her toward him and lifted her thigh, entry was relatively easy despite the obstacle of his protruding tummy. She tried to disguise the moment she'd flinched by playfully biting his neck. She dared herself to look down at the pretty pink water pooling at their feet as he groaned with each gentle thrust.

The water was washing mascara into her eyes, stinging them until she was virtually blind. Her wrist felt like it was breaking as she leant against the wall to keep her balance on one leg. She was trying to turn the water temperature down, trying to blink the black chemicals from her eyes, trying to get her weight off of her wrist, trying to bear the pain of penetration, trying to work out how she could get from here back to her tampons without leaving a trail of blood, trying to do everything other than make love with John.

When he eventually orgasmed inside her she dared to look at the water beneath and was relieved it was still a shade of pink rather than the pool of dark red she was expecting. She kissed him gently and reached for the darker of the two towels on the rail, quickly wrapping it around her and padding back to the toilet for more tissues and tampons.

She looked in the mirror at her bloodshot panda eyes, but she had more pressing matters than to titivate her appearance. The practicalities were on her mind, but it was something else that was now at the forefront. She knew that the lovemaking had not been great for John either. By agreeing to it she had merely infected John with this virus of imperfection.

He was a sensitive lover, and he would be getting dried off alone, knowing that her heart hadn't been in it. He would now know that something was wrong, and it was too late to give him back the perfect memory of tonight that had been his, only half an hour ago.

As she returned to the hallway and wrapped herself in a bathrobe, she became more and more angry with herself. She should have made love whole heartedly or not at all. She had been so distracted by covering her tracks she'd allowed herself to focus on anything other than the love right in front of her. This was not the full extent of her anger, most of all she was angry that her new life with her future husband was starting off with a big fat lie.

That night they slept quietly alongside each other which was in stark contrast to the previous nights when they had slept wrapped around each other. Something had changed and Sophie knew that she had caused it.

She was worried about the affect their lovemaking may have had on her health but decided that none of that was worth what it was doing to her relationship with John.

She hardly slept. The urgency to repair the damage was playing on her mind and as day broke the following morning, she woke him up with breakfast. Everything lovingly halved in the hope that it would be enough of a reminder of their love to dilute any misgivings he had of the night before.

John's mouth spread into a wide grin "Well done!"

She wasn't sure if he was applauding her culinary skills or if he was trying to subtly let her know he'd rumbled her plan for damage limitation, but at least for the time being this seemed to mend the hurt feelings of the previous night.

By comparison to the horrendous start, the next few weeks felt calmer and brighter. She put the inquest to the back of her mind and started to make plans in this new exciting city.

Job hunting in London was an exhausting task, but at least the hotel work was not as seasonal as back home and she found that securing a position as a receptionist was not as difficult as she had imagined. It hardly compared to her previous position of a junior manager but, as John quickly pointed out, this was London, that was Filey and she had, after all been a big fish in a very small pond.

Her periods were back on track and life started to settle down a little but leaving behind family and friends was hard and she missed home terribly.

Sometimes when John worked late and she had the flat to herself for a while, she would give vent to the emotions she didn't want him to see. In this scheduled time of mourning, she would allow herself to travel back in time to those Friday evenings with

Niki and Kelly. The Sunday lunches at her parents' house where they would catch up on the weekly news and make more plans for the ill-fated wedding. She remembered that she was not entirely happy back then but that didn't lessen the feeling of home sickness for a time gone by, and it didn't prevent her crying for the loss of it.

During one such moment of solitary grieving she was startled by the touch of a hand on her shoulder as she knelt on the bedroom floor amid the contents of her memory box.

"Why are you crying?"

"Carl?" She jumped to her feet and spun around frantically to check all directions.

There was silence.

"Carl are you here?"

She knew he was not, and the voice had come from within her own head, but it felt very real at that moment and it was enough to catapult her from nostalgia back into her present world. She blamed the wallowing for triggering this hallucination and vowed never to look back again for the sake of her sanity and her future.

"Never look back unless that's the direction you are going." She repeated her mother's words out loud and headed for the shower to freshen up before John got home.

Cutting herself off from her past this way had never been part of her plan, but right now it felt like protection. Protection from the scorn of those who had known her from birth, protection from the memories she would rather forget, protection from facing her own demons and their infinite power to spoil everything.

John was the one single positive thing to have come from her shattered history and for that reason she nurtured the relationship from dawn until dusk. She loved him dearly, that was never in doubt, but she had become obsessed with making him happy.

Her mother used to say that you will look after something better if you have worked for it, and she had certainly worked for the life she was now living. Worked for it, killed for it and died for it. Losing it all now was not an option, so she worked tirelessly at keeping it safe.

The flat was always immaculate, his friends always welcome, a special meal always ready or in progress, little gifts to make him feel special, romantic nights planned mid-week, expensive lingerie she couldn't afford, and she never ever complained if he was late or wanted to go out with the boys.

She was protecting this love with relentless conviction and it was exhausting. Whenever she found herself at the cash desk with some hideously expensive and impractical diamante encrusted piece of underwear in her hand she didn't falter. A miniscule trinket of trash which she knew would be worn for twenty minutes max was carefully wrapped in pink tissue by the assistant and adorned with sprinkles. She convinced herself that this extravagant behaviour was normal. This is what 'loving your man' should look like.

But as she thrust two twenty-pound notes at the assistant and made a note to cancel her hair appointment to pay for it, she found herself comparing this behaviour to the effortless and relaxed relationship she'd had with Carl. She didn't put much effort into holding onto Carl but that was probably because she didn't love him this much. She took the hideous sparkly bag and walked towards the exit feeling like a desperate fool.

This was not love, this was pure fear. Fear of losing the only positive thing to have been gained from unimaginable misery.

The price tag the assistant had carefully removed from the tiny item, extortionate as it was, could not compete with the price she had already paid for this relationship, and to lose it now and render all the devastation pointless would be an absolute travesty.

After all, there was nothing wrong with keeping the excitement alive and protecting the relationship from harm. She was making sure his eyes were on no-one but her. That his shutters were down. That if a young woman ever spilled the contents of her bag in his path, he would walk over them and trample them into the floor on his way out.

He would be far too occupied with his need to get home to her and her sexy, skimpy, sparkly spoils.

Chapter 20

On a beautiful sunny July day Sophie tossed her overnight bag into the backseat of her car, put on her sunglasses and got into the driving seat. John had bought her the new Fiesta as a run-around to celebrate their engagement. Their flat now had Sophie's mark firmly stamped on it with soft furnishings, rugs and candles in abundance. It was her home now and it felt like home.

She and John were in a good place. It had taken some time, lots of time, but slowly they had rebuilt their relationship and rekindled their love. It seemed that time was indeed a healer and soon there would be no black cloud looming on the horizon. The inquest had finally arrived, and she would soon be on her way to conquer the final hurdle to her inevitable happiness.

She had decided to go alone. It wasn't an act of bravery or a gesture of independence on her part but a need to protect as many people as possible from the event. She didn't want anyone she cared about to hear the abuse and hostility that she was sure was coming her way. Consequently she was leaving John safely in paradise and her parents lives would continue to heal, without the damaging interruption of more drama.

She started her journey with the determination to sail through the ordeal with her composure intact but as the junction numbers of the M1 incremented, her confidence started to diminish and by the time she had progressed to the M18 nerves were getting the better of her.

She pulled in at Junction 5 Services to freshen up, use the toilet and get some sustenance. This was the last motorway service station before she would be transferring to the A and B roads which were less reliable for finding a place to waste the hour of time she needed to. She intended to drive directly to the inquest and had therefore left ample time for any M1 delays.

She turned the radio up to try to distract her on the remainder of her journey to Scarborough Magistrates Court and by the time she parked the car she was feeling in a more positive frame of mind. She gave her name at reception and although she had waited in the car as long as possible the room was not yet ready so she went into the toilets where she could avoid bumping into anyone for the final few minutes. When she returned to the corridor, she could see the doors were open.

She had never been to an inquest before and wasn't sure what to expect but she was relieved to find that the room felt a little less formal than a normal courtroom. The atmosphere, however, was equally daunting, the air thick and heavy with sickly silence. She kept her eyes down as she shuffled to a seat as near to the back as possible to enable her to assess the occupants of the room without walking by any of them.

There were a surprisingly large number of people whom she had never seen before which she found irritating. She thought she knew almost everyone in his life so either she hadn't taken as much interest in him as she should have, or these were just nosey busy bodies, here for the gruesome entertainment of hearing the details of his death.

She recognised his aunt and beside her was a woman who looked a little familiar, but she couldn't quite place her. She was tiny with a mix of black and grey thin dry hair held at the nape of her neck with a black scrunchie. Her thin black nylon coat hung off her bony shoulders causing the sleeves to cover her hands. She looked like a small child who had tried on her mother's coat.

As the woman turned to look over her shoulder Sophie saw dark sunken eyes above protruding cheekbones. Her cheeks were sucked in, giving her face a skull like appearance and her collar bones were clearly visible between the V of the coat neckline.

As Sophie was still trying to remember what was familiar about her, a man's hand slid around the woman's shoulder. The man was Carl's father, and this skeletal woman was all that was left of the chubby, jolly woman that had once been his mother!

This was the woman who used to kiss and hug Sophie every single time they met and who never stopped chatting. The woman who had been so excited that her son was settling down and would give her the grandchildren she was already spoiling in her head. Carl had been their only child. All her dreams were gone.

"Oh, dear lord," Sophie whispered to herself, "what have I done?" Her heart was palpitating wildly and all resolve to sail through what she had described as a mere' last hurdle' had abandoned her.

The inquest was brought to order and the purpose of the occasion was explained to the court. To determine the cause of death and to arrive at a verdict based on the evidence and testimony of both experts and witnesses.

The first to speak was the pathologist who offered medical evidence that the cause of death was due to strangulation. It was explained that hanging which resulted in strangulation was a much longer and more painful process that a hanging from a height in which the cause was more likely to be instant from a broken neck. The reason for making everyone aware of this awful fact seemed to have no purpose other than to deepen the anguish of his parents and to make any perpetrator in the room feel even more wretched than witnessing the demise of his mother.

Sophie's heart, which had started to resume a normal rhythm was jump started again when Niki was called to give evidence. She was near the front and glanced back as she rose from her seat. It was obvious she knew exactly where Sophie was sitting but there was no reassuring smile, her expression was one of contempt.

Thankfully, she gave a brief and impartial account of Carl's reaction to the break-up. Most of her testimony was focussed on the days after Sophie left. The days he didn't bother to go to work or to wash or to eat. The days she had dragged him round to her flat and force fed him, tried to get him to go for a drink with Pete. She was clearly taking the blame for not getting him through this. She was taking the blame for Sophie's crime and thankfully she said nothing about the conversations over Sophie's fantasy lover.

Pete was less merciful in his account of the mess she had left behind as she abandoned Carl to start a new life with her new lover. Several times the judge had to interject and try to keep him to the facts, but he seemed incapable of separating his opinion of the selfish bitch who had done this from the simple events of those days. Although he was repeatedly brought back on track, it was clear to everyone in the room, including the judge, that he was getting great satisfaction from his outbursts.

Sophie fidgeted uneasily as the hatred towards her crept over the courtroom like descending fog. She could feel it building in density and she knew without looking up, that all eyes of this hostile mob were on her. She imagined that at any moment one of them would scream "Burn the witch" and the mob would surge but the sickly silence continued until it was broken gently by a small male voice.

His father spoke of his son's despair at the prospect of spending the rest of his life alone and never having a family because Sophie was the only woman he would want as the mother to his children.

"He told us we would never have a grandchild." He went on and the tears were escaping faster than he could wipe them from his swollen eyes.

His words held no hatred or blame towards Sophie. Nothing but the heart-breaking sadness at the loss of their only son and the grandchildren they would never meet. The palpitations were silenced as anxiety turned to desolation. Her heart was still, she wasn't even sure it was beating any more, frozen in the moment. They were mourning Carl, but they were also mourning the child they would never meet, the child she had flushed away as she drank champagne and partied with John.

As his father finished his gentle account, the courtroom was suddenly blasted with a heart wrenching wail from his mother. It was a sound unlike anything she had heard before, an almost inhuman sound as her legs gave way and her sister tried to support her. So, this is the sound a mother makes at the death of her child. She doesn't dance with champagne in her hand. Sophie was finding it impossible to breathe and at that moment she was called to the stand.

It must have been obvious to everyone in the room that whatever delusions of innocence Sophie had arrogantly carried into this courtroom, they had been knocked out of her by this graphic testimony and spectacle of broken hearts. Endless images of pure grief laid out before her, from her feet to the horizon like the quiet graves of a war memorial burial ground.

None of the questions she was asked were the ones she deserved. Quietly and professionally, she was asked about the day she found Carl. The reason for her visit. Who she had travelled there with and what actions had been taken by her on discovering his body?

She confirmed that there had been no recent communication from her to Carl which might have triggered or caused the event. She hadn't answered any of his texts but that, apparently, is not a crime. It all seemed far too lenient on her. Everyone seemed focussed on what she *did* do when everyone knows that sometimes it's what we *do not* do that causes the damage. Ignoring a person's need to communicate can be a huge blow, sometimes a fatal blow. But delivering a fatal blow by intentionally provoking despair was apparently perfectly acceptable and not worthy of any kind of challenge or retribution.

None of the people with a prerequisite of 'valid interest' chose to question her and for that she was grateful even though she knew that any such questions had to be about the facts alone. Questions they would want to ask like 'how could she live with herself', or 'how deep was her shame' would be disallowed. Tearing someone's heart out and causing their death is perfectly alright but if she had dared to slap his face instead, well for that she would have been arrested.

The verdict was swift and decisive and was recorded as suicide.

The crowd left quietly. No-one suggested burning her alive. They shuffled out defeatedly and respectfully in the firm and certain knowledge that she had got away with murder and there was nothing they could do about it.

Sophie tried to get out before anyone else could reach the door, but a court usher blocked her path and allowed the grieving family to leave before her. She knew the crowd would take a while to disperse so she sat back down to wait until she believed she could leave without being seen.

"Sorry love, you'll have to go now." The same obstructive usher bellowed.

Reluctantly she got up again and made her way back into the foyer. Directly in her path she saw Carl's parents standing with his aunt and uncle. They had their arms around each other for comfort as she was forced to pass close by.

These people she knew well. She had been a much-loved member of this family for so many years. Instinctively she wanted to join the hug, to share her grief with theirs but she knew she was now justifiably ostracised.

Gripped with shame, fear and remorse she tried to hurry past them, but his mother broke from the hug and blocked her escape.

Sophie took a deep breath and prepared to face the wrath she deserved, the punishment she so desperately needed to give her some degree belief that justice had been served.

The two women stood with eyes engaged in a moment of clarity. Sophie wanted to say something, anything to offer some comfort to the lady who had treated her like a daughter. She needed, at least to apologise, to voice her remorse.

She took a breath to speak but before she could form a single word his mother raised a bony finger to her own lips and shook her head gently from side to side. She then stood aside to allow Sophie to leave.

In the years that would follow Sophie thought often of his mother. Of her devastation. The death of the dreams she had of becoming a doting grandmother and sharing the future of her son and his wife but mostly she would be haunted by this final confrontation and the disturbing similarity to the empty note from Carl ….nothing to say.

Chapter 21

Looking back on those early days with John in the millennium year seemed so far removed from the life Sophie was now living.

The years seemed to have passed in the blink of an eye. Years in which they had almost totally removed themselves from their previous northern existence.

The hostility and blame they had endured had resulted in alienation from their roots but had caused them to form a greater bond with each other. In the face of adversity, they had turned their attention inwardly and reduced contact with members of both families.

John's parents had also suffered their fair share of hostility in the town, causing them to leave the house they had chosen for their retirement and relocate several miles inland. Far away from the town where a poor boy had taken his own life due to the recklessness of Sophie Taylor and the arrogant son of the Cardwell's.

They chose to limit all contact with the seaside village as they pretended not to care and concentrated on their own, now perfectly cemented, relationship. Sophie had learned in the first few years to relax and trust John in a way she had never dared to before, and she no longer felt the need to work so hard on romance and sexual gimmicks.

Life was comfortable and the love and commitment between them was surviving admirably. However, the couple in the wedding photo she was now holding in her hand, looked like strangers from another lifetime. She remembered those playful people and the devastation she had felt when her illness had caused her to imagine days where he didn't exist. She also remembered the butterflies in her stomach, now quietened and lifeless, as she tried to console Tori with the 'pretty picture of mummy and daddy'

Tori, now four years old had been frightened once again by Rebecca' s 'bad dream' and the wedding album usually took her mind of it.

"Who's this?"

Tori was still crying and looking with terror through teary black lashes at her sister who sat quietly in the corner. Sophie distracted her by tapping the photo and asking again.

"Mommy" She sobbed as she pushed her dark curls from her own face in order to see Rebecca.

"and?"

Tori cried again.

"and?"

"Daddy."

"Don't they look pretty?"

Tori was nodding and crying alternately as Sophie cuddled her and rocked her to and fro.

John was trying to approach Rebecca to find out what had happened this time. He had an early meeting and didn't need this drama at two am.

Rebecca was sulking. Her sister always went off crying to mum and dad and she was annoyed.

"What happened Rebecca?"

The child sat with her knees tucked up in her night dress, sucking on a strand of her flame red hair. She had turned seven years old a few days before and these 'episodes' seemed to be getting worse.

Eventually she answered her father.

"Nothing. She always cries when I play with Tommy."

John felt anger rising at the mention of this ridiculous imaginary friend, invented by his eldest daughter. It was something she should have grown out of by now and he believed it was nothing more than Rebecca's means of diverting the blame for anything onto a person he could not reprimand.

He knelt before her as he had many times and tried to bully the frail little girl into admitting she had made her sister cry.

"Why is Tori crying?" he asked sharply for the third time since the night had been abruptly interrupted.

Rebecca remained defiant. Her eyes still fixed on the wall ahead of her, her skinny white arms wrapped around her upfolded knees, from which protruded her pale bony feet, lips squeezed tightly together as though someone was trying to force feed her.

"Rebecca!" John was losing patience with his wilful daughter.

"Go back to bed darling," Sophie soothed, "I'll sort them out."

John didn't take up her offer, he was too anxious to sleep.

Tori's terror had subsided into gentle sobs, but still she kept a wary eye on her motionless sister.

Sophie knew that John's anger was not about their disturbed night or his early meeting, it was his way of trying to deny there was anything wrong with Rebecca. He found it easier to pretend his first born was plain naughty than, in any way disturbed.

Sophie tried to endorse John's stance of denial, but secretly she harboured the fear that this imaginary friend might be evidence of her daughter's inability to separate reality from imagination. Evidence that she might have inherited some mental disorder from her mother.

She always tried to get John out of the way when the imaginary friend cropped up in her daughter's explanation for her bad behaviour. She wanted the opportunity to coax Becky into explaining, but John would see that as indulging the child's fabricated excuses and encouraging her to repeat the ridiculous stories.

He was probably right, and Sophie wanted to dismiss these shenanigans with equal fervour, but she could see something in her daughter's eyes that told her this was not a game. The little girl looked up at her as though pleading for help with something she could neither explain nor understand. She silently accepted the wrath of her parents because she had long since given up on being believed.

She feared that Rebecca might be trapped in the horror where reality and dreams coexisted simultaneously. It was a terrifying thought and it filled her with dread whenever another symptom pointed in that direction, but the evidence was building, and she couldn't ignore it. If Rebecca was suffering, it was her job to stand against John and try to help her daughter.

Sophie remembered her own confusion and how she had been unable to cope as an adult so how on earth could a child make any sense of an existence like that? She felt guilty for not publicly validating Rebecca's distraught claims, but she was afraid of where it might all lead. Afraid she might have to reveal her own mental illness to John and the deceit she had maintained for almost a decade.

Even now, even as she watched her fragile little girl trying to recover from John's anger, she couldn't risk it and it wasn't just about the deceit. She couldn't bear for John to know she might have brought this defect into their marriage and infected their child.

Her jealous protection of her relationship was causing her to betray and cruelly abandon her daughter. She sighed deeply. Something was making her tiny daughter ill, lacking in appetite, tired and moody and as clearly as another spot appearing on the face of a child with chicken pox, she knew with each episode that this was a symptom of the very hell she remembered.

She had already taken Rebecca to the doctor a few months earlier at John's insistence, but she had played it down as the poor girl listened to her mother paint the picture of a mildly restless child who had the occasional bad dream.

He consequently recommended they had a quiet story hour before bedtime in a tone that made sure she knew he was annoyed at the wasted time. She smiled and took her daughter's scrawny hand making sure to avoid the eye contact that was being avidly sought. The bewildered child obediently followed the mother who had just let her down.

As they had driven home after the doctor's visit that day, Sophie's heart went out to her troubled, under-nourished child and she decided at least to offer some sort of comfort by humouring her account of the episodes.

Rebecca seemed to come to life at the sheer relief of being able to talk about her friend without being shouted at or called a liar.

Sophie established that Rebecca's dreams were always about a boy called Tommy and that he was not just her friend but her big brother. He was a year older than her and although she called him her brother, she couldn't explain who his parents were or why they were never in her dreams.

"Well how can he be your brother if you don't have the same parents?" she asked light-heartedly

"Dunno," Rebecca replied casually, "I just wanted a brother I think."

Sophie smiled. Perhaps she was making it up after all so as she dropped the little girl back at school and walked back to her car she tried to remember how and when it all started. The first evidence of any strange behaviour from Rebecca had been after Tori was born and she had put it down to jealousy over the fuss being made about a new sister.

She had been only three years old when she suddenly asked where Tommy had gone when she woke up one morning. The poor child had seemed so confused that it was comical and, knowing she had awoken from a dream John and Sophie had found it difficult not to laugh as the toddler checked every corner of their house and then waited at the window for the elusive Tommy.

As time passed, Tommy had become as commonplace as any of the toys spilling annoyingly from the huge toy box in the corner of their lounge, but occasionally John had shown increasing concern over the boy his daughter met in her dreams.

John was now fed up of being woken in the early hours and the assurance from the doctor that she would grow out of it was starting to wear thin.

As he stood up, his expression had mellowed, and he affectionately ruffled the messy red hair which framed a face so pale and gaunt his heart was visibly aching. In stark contrast, the chubby and fully recovered Tori was now squeezing Sophie's nose and laughing which tipped the scale of empathy further in Rebecca's direction.

He passed close to Sophie and put his soft hand gently over hers.

"We have to do something." He whispered.

Sophie nodded and gave his hand a squeeze.

"I know."

Sophie put Tori in bed beside John as she had done many times before, and guided Rebecca back to the girls' room where she put her into bed and got in beside her.

The house returned to normal, but Sophie lay awake planning her next step in trying to determine if her suspicions were accurate. There was only one person she would trust to help her with this discreetly, and she started to conspire a plot to visit her mother in the imminent half term break.

As Rebecca slept, Sophie studied the child's face for any signs of activity, any frowns or smiles that indicated she was somewhere else, some other world from which she might return frightened or, even worse, disappointed.

When, after an hour she had been unable to sleep, she gave up and went back downstairs to make a drink and tidy up the mess they had left in the living room. While she waited for the kettle to boil, she picked up the wedding album and the empty box which had contained the photos. She gathered up the ones she had left strewn across the floor in an attempt to find one that would pacify Tori. She scooped them back into the box, replaced the lid and sat down for a moment with the album.

John, in his smart morning suit was holding his hand over hers as they signed the register. She could still remember the feeling. It had been a nice feeling and it had been a nice day. Nothing wrong with it at all. Her dress had been exactly the one she wanted, and the sun had shone on her as she travelled in her open top car. They had made their vows to each other and meant them. No, nothing wrong with the day at all. In the photo her smile was nice too but that was it, everything was 'nice'.

In reality, it had been a huge disappointment. The photos did not resurrect any butterflies in the pit of her stomach because there hadn't been any. Maybe it was because they decided to have the ceremony in London out of respect for Carl's family back in Filey, or maybe it was because the guests were mostly made up of people she had known for only a year from her new job and a few friends of John's that she hardly knew.

Apart from her parents, no-one from her family had made the journey, and nor had any of her old school friends. In short, both Niki and Kelly had politely declined the invitations with no reason given. She had tried to console herself by using the distance as the probable cause but underneath that sticking plaster was the ugly sore of conspiracy and solidarity from her hometown, as though the word 'bitch' had been scrawled over her wedding car.

She stroked John's smiling face on the shiny photograph and wondered if he had felt the same as her, or if his smile was the deep felt happiness he had dreamed he would feel on his wedding day. Either way, she loved him. She loved him if his smile was genuine and, if he was faking it for her sake, she loved him even more. Her finger followed the contour of his neck and chest down to their joined hands on the register. She loved her husband as she had never loved before and that surely had to make the day as perfect as it could have been. Yes, it had been a nice day, nothing wrong with it at all.

She flicked over the pages to their first dance to "This Guy's in love with you" and a genuine smile awakened her tired face. He had chosen the song as it was the one he had sung to her often when he was feeling romantic and it had become 'their song' She thought it was probably the only song he knew the words to. It was also slow enough for him to remember them in time, and that made her smile too.

He had held her so proudly as he waltzed her around that room with his hand gently but firmly in the small of her back. Music started playing in her head as she imagined them dancing again on that huge dance floor alone, but the tune wasn't right. It was not their song at all, it was "Tonight I celebrate my love!" That was not a song she had ever shared with John! Still, it played on in her head and the voice that was softly singing along was Carl's.

"Do you remember our song baby?" A voice whispered from behind her.

"Go away!" she snapped out loud as she spun around with the photograph to her chest as though protecting it from the intrusion. She felt angry not frightened, angry that her mind was playing tricks again, angry that the nightmare might be returning.

There was no-one behind her. No spectre of Carl but she wanted to blame him rather than accept that the horror was seeping from within her own mind. She took a stride forward into the exact place she believed the voice had come from to demonstrate that she held no fear of him.

"Why don't you just fuck off and leave me alone?" She barked at the space she now occupied. There was no response other than the gentle bubbling of the kettle.

She bundled the photographs back into the cabinet and poured the tea, wrapped her dressing gown tightly around her for comfort and sat with her legs tucked under her in the armchair and waited for sleep to speed her into the following day.

John's kiss on the top of her head startled her into noticing the terrible crick in her neck from sleeping in the chair.

"Why are you down here Soph?"

"Just fell asleep." She half yawned while gently moving her head in circles to loosen the tense muscle.

"It's probably nothing too serious going on with Becks you know." He soothed rumpling her already dishevelled hair.

"I know." She lied patting his hand, "she's likely seen something on TV that's started the nightmares of this Tommy character. We do need to get to the bottom of it though."

"Yes, I know we do."

Sophie got up and walked to the kettle suddenly feeling very unattractive and grubby. John was already washed and dressed and here she was with a flat patch of hair at the back of her head, unwashed sweaty body, stale teeth and rancid breath. She wouldn't blame him if he didn't want to be close to her at all. She took refuge in the tea making and tried to avoid close contact with him. Even after all these years, it mattered to her that she was attractive to John, that she was his sexy lover as well as his wife and mother to his children.

"I've been thinking of taking the girls to see mum and dad next week if that's ok?"

There was a silence Sophie knew was coming. She never took the girls to Filey if she could avoid it. It was as though she was ashamed to visit her hometown which she believed, still harboured the same resentment against them. She wanted to keep the children away from the judgmental attitude of the small community who mourned the loss of Carl like he had been their local hero.

"What for?"

"I just thought a change of scenery may help Rebecca," she lied, "break the routine maybe?"

John didn't really need to know her reasons, he was just pleased she seemed to be trying to face this fear that the entire population of her home town were still grieving for Carl and still waiting to vent their anger on her with their everlasting hatred.

"Good idea. Do you want me to see if I can get a few days off and come with you?"

"No. It's fine. I'll have a bit of girly time with mum if I can."

She kept her face away from him as she poured the milk partly because she didn't want him to look too closely at her tired naked face but mainly because he would know immediately that there was something else. John knew every tiny muscle in her expressions, and he would know there was more to this.

"Ok." He said cheerily, walking over to pick up his tea and giving her buttock a squeeze.

She flinched slightly. "Stop it, I'm a mess!"

"Yes you are," he teased, "but you are my mess." He squeezed her again and this time she turned towards him and hugged him gently, sliding her hands under his jacket and around his middle which was even greater than when she had met him, and she loved him even more.

"That's my girl" he smiled, "and.....?"

She sighed "That's my guy." She confirmed, smiling contentedly that he needed the reassurance even today.

"Can I make daddy's toast?" Rebecca asked from behind the hugging couple.

"Of course," John winked at her, "yours is better than mum's."

Rebecca seemed to have no knowledge of the previous night's trauma and happily popped the bread in the toaster while arranging a plate and knife on the table.

"She's going to be fine." John winked again but this time at his wife.

Sophie nodded.

On the Sunday night the girls were both excited about their trip to nan and grandad's and wanted to go to bed early to make the morning come faster.

"Can we play on the sand?" Tori asked for the hundredth time since Sophie had told them.

"Stop asking that!" Sophie snapped as she started to get irritated by the frivolity and silliness. This trip was not about buckets and spades but about seeking our Dr Walker and burdening him with the horrific update since her last visit. If anyone could help Rebecca without attaching a stigma to her, she hoped he was the one.

"Tommy is off school this week too" Rebecca announced, oblivious to the reception her comment would get.

Sophie chose to ignore it, but her heart was sinking fast.

Tori's face was starting to crumple as though she was going to cry.

Sophie had to intervene without confrontation.

"Most schools have the same holiday but you two are going to be at the seaside this week. I can take you to the amusements and the donkeys. It will be fun."

"Donkeys?" Rebecca was sufficiently distracted from the wretched Tommy's plans but Sophie's decision to seek advice was further reinforced and the sooner the better.

A few days later she was heading north while trying to entertain two squabbling children from the driving seat. She had never made such a long journey as the sole adult and it was proving quite a challenge. Books made them feel sick, Tori was too young for 'I spy' , drinks and snacks had been consumed long before the M1 and she had resorted to extending the journey by pulling in at almost every service station to play on teddy grabbing machines and buy cheap trinkets that would go straight in the bin the moment they arrived.

She had hoped to have time to plan on how to approach the entire subject with her mum and to explain why she hadn't told her any of it before now, but by the time she turned onto the country roads towards her hometown she was totally exhausted. At last, she turned onto the lane where she had played happily as a child and an ache gripped her, a sadness that reminded her of a previous life. A life she had always believed her own children would share in this holiday town full of summer life and winter tranquillity.

The life they had in Chelmsford was a world away from candy floss, shell collecting and fish and chips and although she loved their house, their friends, the dinner parties, the corporate hospitality she couldn't shake this feeling of regret that Rebecca and Tori had not experienced or shared her roots.

As she pulled up outside her childhood home, her mum and dad were waiting at the door just as she expected they would be, and the girls ran up the path to the cottage they had only visited a couple of times before.

Most family get-togethers had taken place in Chelmsford and although John always made them feel so very welcome, Sophie knew that they were far from comfortable in his world and felt inferior despite John's own humble beginnings.

This was a real treat to have them visit, and although it was unusual, they had not questioned the purpose of it all, they were just happy that it was happening, and they could at last introduce their only grandchildren to the delights of Yorkshire life.

Over the obligatory cup of tea Sophie noticed her mum's hair was styled differently, that none of her clothes looked familiar and concluded that it had been far too long since she had seen them in person. Dad took the girls for a walk along the beach which gave her the opportunity she had been longing for, the chance to offload this burden she had carried for so very long. She sat at the kitchen table and sighed.

"What is it Sophie? Is everything alright? Where's John?"

Immediately her mother was jumping to conclusions about the unusual visit.

"John's fine. It's Becky I'm having trouble with but first there's something I need to tell you and I don't know where to start."

Christine knew her daughter well enough to see that this was no small matter, so she made the obligatory pot of tea and returned to the table.

"Let's start at the beginning Sophie. I'm listening."

Consequently, Sophie commenced to spill out the whole story, from her own first strange dream to the last episode with Rebecca.

Her mum sat in silence as the years of heartache, joy, despair and guilt unfolded in her tiny kitchen. She watched her daughter's transcending emotions like she was watching a film on tv, no reaction, no words, no gestures of comfort, she just listened and watched.

Sophie could see that her mother was absorbing every detail, probably shocked that all this had happened to her only child without her noticing or getting a single hint that anything was wrong. She heard about the fantasy of her own brain tumour, and her daughter's imaginary suicide without a single change of expression in the 'middle distant stare' she had held from the very first sentence.

Eventually Sophie reached the point at which she had decided to seek out her old doctor. She took a breath, and all was quiet, her voice silenced, her expressions stilled on her tear-stained face. Christine looked at her daughter for a few moments and then said.

"You aborted Carl's child?"

It wasn't a question it was a reprisal of the utmost order. It was the only fact from the whole disturbing story that she had chosen to discuss, and Sophie starred back in disbelief.

Christine ran her hand despairingly through her curled hair, inhaled and then pushed the air back out in an enormous sigh.

She looked again at this young woman in front of her and Sophie returned the stare. It was a pivotal moment between mother and child, a moment that could never be undone or rewritten and they both knew it. Sophie was testing her mother's support to the limit and Christine was wrestling with her conscience and her faith in her daughter's sanity.

Eventually the silence was broken by Christine.

"Oh Sophie." Her tone was soft as she reached across the table and took her daughter's hands in hers.

Sophie sighed with relief. The verdict was in and it had gone in her favour.

"Will you help me mum?"

"Of course."

"Do you think Rebecca is ill?"

"No!" Christine's tone was firm. "She is not ill, and neither are you. We'll make an appointment with the doctor tomorrow. He's still practising and I'm sure he will see you even though you are out of the catchment area. I'm sure he'll say it's just a phase and no connection to your own vivid dreams when you were stressed to death, wrestling with the decision over a marriage you didn't want"

Sophie smiled weakly "I've already made a private appointment; I went to see him years ago about the same thing."

"Did you? What did he say?" Christine's tone was relaxed.

"He said I had a sleep disorder. Same thing the doctor back home said about Rebecca, but hers seems to be getting worse."

"Well, I kind of hoped your visit was because you were missing us, but I'll take what I can get," she laughed to lighten the mood a little, "I'll come with you. Your dad can watch Tori for an hour."

It was all very well sharing this with her mother but the following day, when it actually came to walking into the doctor's surgery with Rebecca she felt very differently. Making a private appointment from her five bedroomed country house with John's credit card felt empowering and dignified but here in the waiting room of her home town surgery with her mum by her side and her child on her knee she felt inferior, stupid and belittled.

She was no longer the well-heeled wife of an affluent company director paying for private therapy, she was little

Sophie Taylor sitting in Dr Walker's waiting room with her mum. She should have known better than to come back here, where returning to your previous life also means adopting your previous status. No wonder celebrities never go home.

By the time she entered the surgery she could feel the danger of being labelled a mental patient looming in the air.

"Yes?" Dr Walker greeted her in the same way he had many years ago, peering over his reading glasses.

Sophie felt ridiculously nervous as she stammered and stuttered through the symptoms Rebecca was displaying and the trauma of her nightmares of the imaginary Tommy.

"Could it be something hereditary?" Sophie asked, "it's very similar to the problem you treated me for isn't it?"

The doctor looked puzzled and tried to consult the screen in front of him by banging a selection of keys and then frowning to assess the result of his bombardment. He was obviously struggling with the technology that he had most likely been bullied into using to avoid being forced into retirement.

"What exactly did I treat you for?" He was still peering at the screen as though willing it to spontaneously enlighten him.

"You said it was a sleep disorder. Back in 2000? – Yes definitely 2000. February, I think."

He frowned again "Well there is nothing on here about it," he looked up at her and grinned, "there's not much about anything on here if the truth be known."

"Well do you remember seeing me?" Sophie wasn't in the mood for humour.

The doctor smiled, "I can't remember the ones I saw last week let alone years ago but no I'm afraid I don't recall it. I could get someone to check the paper files though, in case it got missed?"

Sophie sighed. She knew that would take days and tried to think of something that might jog his memory.

"You told me that my dreams would have no colours or tastes remember? You were trying to prove to me that John, my new boyfriend, wasn't real?"

Sophie stared at Dr Walker and he stared back. His moment of contemplation was an attempt to flick through the archives of his memory and find the missing conversation. Sophie's moment of contemplation was the trepidation at realising that her previous appointment had not been in this existence.

The silent stare continued until Sophie suddenly flushed with embarrassment and needed to cover her tracks.

"Never mind. I just want you to help Rebecca."

The old man took off his worn suit jacket and leant forward towards the frail little girl before him.

"So, Rebecca, tell me about Tommy. Is he your friend?"

She nodded mistrustfully winding a saliva-soaked curl of hair around her finger

"Where does he live?"

"I don't know."

"Does he come to your house?"

"I don't know." She looked up at the old man who raised his eyebrows expectantly, "I don't think so." She nestled more closely to Sophie for reassurance.

"Can you see him now?"

The child looked shocked and offended.

"Of course not. He isn't here!" she seemed almost amused by the suggestion.

"Do you ever see him when nobody else can?"

She looked at Sophie as though this man was stupid.

"No. Everybody sees him when he's here."

The doctor smiled and turned to Sophie.

"She doesn't have an imaginary friend. She is just remembering a dream. Sometimes dreams seem very real to children"

Sophie knew he would say that. It had been a waste of time and she decided that the only person who could help Rebecca was herself and what was worse was that she would have to keep it from everyone else. Everyone except her mum who would become her single confidant.

She was reminded of something Niki once said. "Your mother is the only person in the world who is always completely on your side" How true that was, and she knew she had to be on Rebecca's side. She also knew that she missed Niki terribly. She knew she could never share any of this with John and she knew that right now she needed to get out of this place.

She stood up and thanked the doctor enthusiastically as though he had solved her problem and pulled open the heavy door dragging Rebecca behind her. Back in the waiting room, she knelt before the child and smiled.

"Everything is going to be alright, Becky. Are you ready to ride a donkey?"

Amid Rebecca's squeals of delight, she could hear the voices whispering in the surgery as the old oak door closed far too slowly. She suspected her mother of voicing concerns behind her back, but she didn't have the energy for a confrontation today. She would say nothing, but she had made a mental note that there may be an element of disloyalty emerging and that her mother may be paying lip service to her problem whilst secretly harbouring doubts about her sanity.

Chapter 22

As they made their way back to the car, Rebecca chatted happily as she skipped along holding grandma's hand, but Sophie was deep in contemplation. The conversation with the doctor had caused her to recollect the alleged visit in 2000 and how vivid the memory was, not like a dream at all, and she was shaken at being reminded just how real this double existence had actually been.

She shuddered and then looked over at Rebecca. If her little daughter was experiencing the same thing then just how terrifying it must be, and how terribly lonely she must feel. She didn't yet have adequate communication skills to explain this to an adult. The poor girl must be in a living nightmare.

She felt the need to hold her, so she moved alongside and put her arm around the skeletal child.

As the three of them walked along the sea front in the direction of the car park they passed by Sophie's old flat. She tried not to look up put couldn't seem to stop herself. Christine noticed immediately and tried to distract her.

"What shall we have for dinner tonight then?"

Sophie was still staring up at the window of the place where she had found Carl hanging from the ceiling. Her pace slowed as she scanned the boarded-up windows and vandalised door. The whole building was abandoned and looked as though it had been vacated many years ago.

"Come on slow coach." Rebecca laughed as she tugged at Sophie's limp hand. The meagre tug from her daughter could hardly be felt although she seemed to be putting every bit of her frail strength into it.

As she walked, Sophie fumbled in her handbag for the car keys and her expression became serious and distant. She separated two keys from the bunch and toyed with them.

"They aren't.....?" Christine asked.

"Yup. My old keys."

"Don't even think about it!"

Sophie was already moving towards the edge of the pavement with the keys in her hand.

"What good is this going to do?" Christine was becoming more anxious by the second.

"I just need to see it. The locks have probably been changed and other people will have lived there since."

"No-one has lived there," her mum snapped, "it was already rundown and there was a plan for a complete renovation. A company put in an offer to convert it into fancy apartments for young professionals but, well after the suicide, the offer was withdrawn, and they developed a block in Scarborough instead."

"You mean it's still how we left it?"

"I imagine so. The last few residents moved out a few years after and the landlord moved to Spain. No idea what's happening to it."

"I need to go back." She said firmly as she let go of Rebecca's hand and stood at the kerb waiting for a gap in the traffic.

Christine held onto her Granddaughter's hand tightly.

"We'll wait here."

Rebecca was sensing something was strange and had a sudden interest in the conversation.

"I want to come too. Let me come too." She was trying to writhe her hand free from her grandmother's.

"It's Ok. She can come," Sophie soothed "it will have been cleared out by now."

Rebecca broke loose as soon as Christine released her grip and ran to Sophie's side. As they crossed the road Christine followed a few steps behind but as Sophie placed the key in the lock and turned it. Christine stood back to wait. To everyone's surprise, the door opened.

The flight of stairs looked hugely different. The paint had peeled from the iron banister and the wallpaper above the dado rail hung in damp strips, some of which were almost touching the steps before her. The door to their flat however, looked exactly the same and as she tried the other key, a tiny click caused her heart to skip a beat.

Tentatively, Sophie pushed the door back and stepped inside with Rebecca close behind. The flat was dark and smelled musty. As her eyes adjusted to the dimly lit room Sophie gasped a little.

"What's the matter mummy?" Rebecca whined.

"Nothing darling." Sophie was absorbing the scene before her. Nothing had changed. Nothing at all. It seemed like the flat had been boarded up that very night and nothing had been removed. There was still a shopping list on the hall table. Milk, tea bags, orange cordial and potatoes. She felt sick. In the small kitchen the pots were still in the sink, Carl's last meal. Her knees were so weak that she could hardly put one foot in front of the other.

"Mummy! Look in here." Rebecca had set off exploring and opened the door into the bedroom.

"Come out of there!!" Sophie shouted as she ran across the living room to the door through which her daughter had disappeared.

Rebecca was holding a teddy bear; the one Carl had bought her on their first Christmas and Sophie's throat closed as she tried again to speak. She swallowed hard.

"Put that back!"

"Who lives here mummy?"

"Nobody. It will be knocked down soon."

"I hope not" Rebecca sounded concerned.

"It's not anyone's home anymore."

"It used to be though."

"Yes. A long time ago."

Sophie was herding Rebecca back through the bedroom door when she noticed the brown stains on the walls. The blood had turned to mud-like patches. Patches of desperation. Testimony to a terrifying irreversible change of mind as Carl fought for air. Seeped into the walls of their happy home, were patches of Carl.

"Did Tommy live here?"

Sophie became irritated that Rebecca was trying to bring the imaginary friend back into play.

"Of course not!"

"I think he used to live here because I played here with him here a long time ago."

The shock of the gruesome patches didn't compare to the blood that was now draining from Sophie face or the chills down her spine that Rebecca was relating to this place. She scooped up the child and hurried blindly back through the bedroom door. With Rebecca blocking her view she crashed straight into the figure that blocked her path to the stairway. She screamed. Rebecca screamed.

"Oh my God!" Christine gasped. "What on earth?"

"Let's just get out of here." Sophie gasped as she tried to recover from the collision, the fear, and the confusion of the last few minutes.

"I told you this was a bad idea. What were you thinking?" Christine slammed the door behind them.

Sophie ran to the car and put Rebecca in the back seat. She then got into the driving seat and held her hands up to cover her face. She couldn't talk about it, couldn't bear to think about it, but the worst thing of all was the uneasy feeling she had about Rebecca's reaction to the flat, and the belief that she had been there before. She breathed deeply but her heart was racing, and it was taking every bit of her resolve to fight sheer panic.

Gently she started the car and drove back to her parent's house with the distant chatter of child and grandma in the background. Not a single word spoken between the pair of them, had registered in Sophie's overloaded brain.

That evening she put Rebecca and Tori to bed and sat watching TV with mum and dad, just wishing the hours to pass so she could go to bed herself and give her mind a rest from the images of the day.

That night she could hear Rebecca talking to Tommy in her sleep again and Tori kept waking up because of it. After a couple of visits to the children's room to resettle them Sophie couldn't make any more polite conversation. She needed to be alone and asked if her mum minded watching the children while she went for a walk.

"Do you want me to come with you?"

"No!" her response was excessively abrupt, "no thanks. I really want a few minutes alone"

"Ok." Her mother sounded hurt but didn't try to dissuade her.

Sophie left the house wearing only jeans and tee shirt even though the night air felt chilly. She had been too desperate for solitude to seek out a jumper. Out in the night air, she walked along the country lanes she had frequented as a child. She knew every bend in the road, every tree and bush that lined the gravel lane. How happily she had ridden her bicycle along this lane with Kelly, packed up with a bottle of orange and a cheese sandwich on an adventure over the fields and woods. How simple life had seemed.

For the first time, she understood the innocence of a child. Those wonderful years when no serious mistakes had yet been made and the conscience was totally clear. When no regrets had yet taken up residence in the heart, preventing it from flying free and no heavy burden of guilt was to be carried, until the last breath would finally allow it to be put down.

She marched purposefully as she fought back the tears. The rain started to fall gently, and the dampness of her clothes felt strangely comforting. Turning off the lane and onto a familiar meadow she ran for a short while and then fell to the ground under a solitary tree. As a child she had named it the lightening tree after the song from Folly foot. Many an hour she had sat under this tree making pictures from the clouds and wiling away the summer days while singing that familiar song.

Today the tree felt hostile and judgemental of her lost innocence. It was like returning to a respected teacher in shame of the mess she had made of all she had been taught.

She sat, deep in thought, beneath the old tree for quite some time. Thoughts with no order or purpose. Just a muddle of random events and emotions hitting her one after the other like the relentless beat of a deafening disco. She held her hands to her ears as though shutting out the noise from within and heard a noise bellow from her own mouth which was almost a howl. The pain from within her had finally found a vent of release.

As she peered back into the darkness from where she had come, she could vaguely see the outline of a figure. Stifling her howl, she tried to focus on the person standing beside the lane. Maybe her father? Could it be Carl still haunting her? Slowly she rose to her feet and started to walk back towards the lane and the mysterious figure. She felt no fear, she was beyond fear, beyond concern for her own safety, beyond reason.

Purposefully she marched through the falling rain occasionally pushing her wet hair back from her rain-soaked face.

"Sophie?" Her heart stood still.

"John? Oh, thank God. John!"

She fell into his arms like a lost child into the arms of a searching father.

"Baby, what are you doing?" He held her tightly against him as he wrapped his coat around her.

"I don't know," she sobbed, "how did you even get to be here"

"You called me."

"No, I didn't." she frowned.

John smiled in only the way he could "Your heart called me."

She looked up at him and the tears of despair were replaced by tears of relief and gratitude.

"Thank God our hearts can talk then." she sighed.

"Thank God indeed."

They walked back in silence without letting go of each other for an instant.

Chapter 23

Later that night, after a hot shower and a hot chocolate they kissed the children good night together and cuddled up close in bed. Sophie slept more soundly that night than she had for months and still she didn't let go of John's hand for a single second.

The next day they returned home, and Sophie divulged that she had taken Rebecca to the doctor who had said she was only 'going through a phase.' It didn't feel like a lie because she had already convinced herself that this was the case.

John just shrugged in a disgruntled but defeated manner as he poured himself his evening gin and tonic.

In the distance, Sophie could hear Rebecca whispering and although she tried to ignore it for a few minutes she was worried that John might hear it. Many times, she had tried to disguise Rebecca's ramblings. It felt like her own shame. An imperfection she needed to hide from the man whose admiration she still craved.

As John sat down with the paper, she stirred a couple of pots on the cooker before disappearing into the hallway and up the stairs. Rebecca was sat bolt upright with her eyes wide open whispering frantically to herself. It was difficult to get the gist of what she was saying but it seemed as though she were telling her imaginary friend how to wake someone.

"Shake her, shake her!" she urged, "put water on her face, that will wake her up."

Rebecca stopped to listen to the reply which only she could hear and then she looked disappointed.

"Never mind." She soothed as she extended her arms to comfort her companion.

"Rebecca?" Sophie whispered.

"What?"

"Rebecca darling you are dreaming."

Rebecca frowned a little and didn't resist as Sophie settled her back down to sleep the way she did many times a week.

She kissed Rebecca gently and then turned to Tori who was sleeping soundly as her lips sucked the imaginary dummy which had been thrown away almost two years ago. It still made Sophie smile. She took a final look at her beloved children before returning to the man she loved. Life was good and she felt a surge of optimism and general wellbeing about the life she had finally carved out for herself.

Dinner went pretty much the same way as most evenings, with a couple of glasses of wine and a lively humorous conversation with John. She loved how they still made each other laugh after all these years. How they still made time for a private dinner a couple of times a week. At one point they were unable to swallow the food for laughing and she loved the way his tubby belly heaved with each gasp.

After dinner they made love on the sofa before going to bed holding hands. She never took their love for granted and marvelled every single day at how the strength of it had not once wavered since that very first moment he flashed his cheeky smile in her direction. Many times, they would jointly relive those first dates and cringe as they recalled making love in the car on the first night they met.

She snuggled in beside him and closed her eyes contentedly. The night would have been perfect were it not for the distant whispering. She kept her eyes shut for a moment, hoping that Rebecca would go back to sleep, but the voice was getting louder and it felt like she was being approached by her sleepwalking daughter.

"Mummy. Mummy," the voice was soft but didn't sound like Rebecca, "Wake up Mummy."

It was a child's voice, but Sophie couldn't seem to open her eyes. Her eye lashes were welded together as though glued. She used every muscle in her face to try to peel them apart as the child's voice continued to gain excitement.

"Mummy! Mummy!" it squealed, "Daddy come quick."

She tried again to open her eyes, but they felt like they were still welded shut and her hands were so heavy she could hardly lift them to rub at her sealed lids. This was a whole new level of haunting.

Then as one eye reluctantly yielded to her painful fingers, it opened slightly. Just enough for her to catch a partly focussed glimpse of a little blonde boy running away down a white corridor.

She turned to wake John, but he had disappeared along with the other half of the bed she had fallen asleep in. Her out-flung arm hit a metal rail of the single bed.

She tried to shout, but her throat hurt so badly and seemed to be blocked.

"Sophie?" This was a voice she knew – it was the ghost of Carl again. She closed her eyes tightly and prayed to be released from the nightmare but as she opened them again, Carl's face came slowly but surely into view.

"Sophie baby. Oh, thank God, thank God!"

She had no idea what he was thanking God for and tried blinking several times to be rid of him.

Carl was crying as he hugged the little blonde boy.

"Mummy is awake Tommy. She's awake again!"

Could this really be Carl? He looked different. As if someone had drawn around his eyes and roughed up his complexion. Could he have survived after all and where had he been? She thought of the inquest, the sheer weight of his body in her arms, she was sure he was dead, of course he was dead yet here he was smiling at her but looking very different.

Her mind was racing out of control as she searched madly for John once again. Did he call the little boy Tommy a moment ago? Could this be Rebecca's imaginary friend but why was he here? And where was Rebecca now? And where was John? She had to find John! Her heart was pounding at the idea that she may be in an old nightmare again and if so, it felt every bit as real as it had long ago.

She let out a scream from the pit of her stomach. It was hardly audible, but it brought a man in a white coat hurrying over. He immediately herded Carl and the boy away from the remaining half of her marital bed.

The doctor approached and took her hand. "Do you know where you are?"

Sophie shook her head still scanning the room for John or Rebecca.

"You are in the hospital. You have been here for quite some time."

"But...but.." Her voice was a squeaky whisper.

"Don't try to talk. You need to rest."

Sophie was already panicking. The girls were still in bed and she was wondering if they had been in a house explosion in their sleep that had put them all in hospital, but she couldn't make sense of the appearance of Carl and the little boy, unless she had been hallucinating.

The doctor sat quietly beside her with a woman she did not recognise, although she looked reassuringly comforting.

"This is Anne. She is a psychologist."

"What?" Sophie whispered, panic escalating as she fought to get the words out through a dry swollen throat.

"Is it bad news? She gasped, "are Rebecca and Tori alright?" Every syllable was an effort.

A concerned look passed back and forth between doctor and psychologist ending in a synchronised frown.

"You need to rest a while?" The doctor seemed confused and concerned

"No! Please just tell me what's happened" She whispered, feeling more terrified each time she heard the barely recognisable sounds coming from her own mouth.

The lady known as Anne leaned forward, she wasn't that old but there was something strangely motherly about her, her round rosy face framed by black curls gave her the air of a farmer's wife. Devoid of fashion sense, self-indulgence or ego, a homemaker, a mother hen, a do-gooder if you like but she smelled of soap and her chubby hand on Sophie's was warm and calming.

"You have been ill for a very long-time love."

"Ill? I haven't been ill." Sophie croaked again holding her throat with both hands as though trying to force the sounds out.

"Yes, you have love. You have been in a coma."

"A coma? For how long?"

Anne looked at the doctor who nodded his approval.

"An exceptionally long time Sophie. You have been in a coma for nine years."

Sophie laughed out loud.

"Don't be stupid. I put the kids to bed only a few hours ago."

"What kids?" Anne asked softly as she patted the hand she was still holding very gently.

"My daughters, Rebecca and Tori."

"Listen Sophie. This is a lot to take in and the doctor is going to give you a little sedation until you have the time to absorb all of this at a pace you can cope with."

"I don't need sedation I need to know what's going on." Sophie was crying.

Anne put her arms around Sophie's frail shoulders.

"You had an accident a long time ago and fell into a coma but by some miracle today you came back, and everyone is thanking God that you are awake again. Your family is thrilled but it's too much for you to take in all at once."

"Where's John?" was all Sophie could sob, "where's John?"

No-one answered this question. No-one could. Everyone was being wonderful and kind in the most patronising way possible.

As she lay in her hospital bed watching the expressions of nurses and doctors, she knew these were the expressions of those humouring a mad woman. Smiling and nodding and patting her arm sympathetically. It was not sympathy for the fact that she could not find her family or that she worried for her children, it was the sympathy extended to those who were deluded, and it was sickening.

Anne was the only person who seemed to give her any credibility and, in this respect, she seemed like a lifeline in this new world of hideous insanity.

In the hours that followed, desperately Sophie told her about her life with John and their daughters, their home and the schools they attended as though she were a lost child trying to give a policeman her name and address in the hope of being instantly returned.

She even detailed the dinner she had cooked the previous night and their plans for a holiday as if this might somehow speed her return journey.

Anne had a way with her, it was difficult to explain, but Sophie trusted her and when Anne had finished listening to the story, she didn't smile condescendingly she looked at Sophie in a serious manner and spoke firmly.

"I know all that feels very real to you, but you have been asleep for an awfully long time and you need to try to understand all of this a bit at a time. As the days pass it will start to sink in and you will be able to start to rebuild your life."

Sophie covered her ears and shook her head violently.

"You are as bad as the others!"

Anne took her hands and pulled them gently from her ears.

"Look." She said as she pulled back the bed sheets.

"What?"

Anne was nodding towards Sophie's legs.

Sophie stared at the skinny pale limbs almost as white as the sheets themselves. They were not her legs; they were pathetic little sticks of flesh-covered bone.

She looked up to Anne who was nodding gently with tears in her eyes.

Sophie began shake from head to toe.

"What happened to me? Oh God, what happened to me?"

Anne held her close and this time the smell of soap was not so comforting, but she was pleased for the hug as it filled a little bit of time in which she could stop thinking.

"You have been in a coma Sophie. Do you understand?"

This time Sophie nodded her head which was still buried in Anne's neck.

Anne pulled away and looked her in the eyes again.

"You have been in a coma and the doctors knew you still had brain activity because they were measuring it. There was lots of activity and that was probably the dreams you were having. You have had years and years of dreams, Sophie and to you that must feel like you have lived a whole life."

Sophie was still nodding as though she was accepting every word, but she still couldn't make sense of it.

"But you are back now, and your family are so, so happy. You do remember them, don't you?"

"I remember Carl." She whispered.

"Well, that's a start."

"Who is the boy? Did Carl get married?"

Anne smiled "This is the good part Sophie. You were pregnant when you had your accident, and the doctors delivered your son while you were here."

"That was my son?"

"I know it's a lot to take in but yes, he is your son, and he has visited you since he was a baby. Your boyfriend has brought him every week or so to see you and has sat and talked with you, Carl always believed you could hear him"

Sophie looked up in bewilderment.

"I think I did from time to time." The reality was slowly sinking in as she remembered him whispering to her that they were having a baby and the song he was singing as she looked through her wedding album.

"What kind of accident did I have?"

"That doesn't matter now." Anne soothed

"It does to me."

"You did something very silly. You took an overdose."

Sophie remembered the shed floor, the terror of it, her desperate attempt to make herself sick. Her head hitting something and the gushing hot blood.

This was all too much to take in. If she wasn't already mad, she was sure this would send her totally insane. She closed her eyes and visualised John, his cheeky grin, his sincere eyes, his strong arms around her. He was real. She remembered every detail of her lovely girls, their faces and smiles. Their frowns and sulky expressions, the feel and smell of their hair and skin.

Only a few hours ago she had been with her family, holding them, touching them and talking with them. She wanted to sleep, to escape and to forget she had ever had this bloody awful dream and met this condescending Anne who seemed hell bent on tearing her world apart.

"I want to rest now." She lied as she attached every morsel of hope on disappearing from this nightmare, through the worm hole sleep might provide.

"Of course," smiled Anne "I don't think you should see your family until you are strong enough to relate to them properly."

"No, I don't want to see anybody yet." Sophie agreed.

"Your little boy has waited his whole life to meet his mummy and to disappoint him could damage your relationship with him forever."

Sophie didn't care one bit about the stupid boy's disappointment, but it was her turn to humour Anne.

"Of course. He won't be disappointed. I just need to come to terms with all of this."

Anne seemed a little sceptical at the sudden turnaround and Sophie knew that Anne was no fool, but it didn't matter. Nothing in this weird place mattered, including the suggestion that she had a son, for very soon she would be back down the worm hole and waking up safely beside her beloved John.

Chapter 24

The sound of clattering pots and cheery greetings woke her as the day swung into action on ward 22. Sophie opened her eyes to find a young woman smiling at her with a cup of tea.

Disappointment and terror rose simultaneously through her body like an erupting volcano. She heard the cup and saucer crash to the floor as she whacked it out of the poor woman's hand in frustration.

Immediately nurses were upon her, restraining her and calling for sedation.

"I'm sorry, I'm sorry!" was all she could mutter, in an attempt to reassure the descending mob that she wasn't dangerous, but it was too late, she felt the pressure of the needle in her arm and she was drifting somewhere outside of her body in a place she didn't need to think.

The next thing she remembered was the familiar smell of fresh soap and the strangely reassuring voice of Anne.

"I know this is frightening for you," Anne whispered, "but you have to try to accept what is real, and the sooner you can do that the sooner you are going to start to feel able to pick up your life."

If this was truly reality, then Sophie knew she was right, but how could she accept this as her reality when her other life was every bit as real as this?

"Perhaps a visitor would help? Someone you could talk to other than your partner or son?"

Sophie tried to think of someone who's reality or otherwise would be obvious to her

"My mum. Can you get my mum to come?"

Anne covered her face with her hands for a moment and seemed to sigh.

"What is it?"

Anne stroked her head as though comforting a sick child.

"Do you remember your mum being ill?"

Sophie's heart sank "Yes she had a brain tumour." As she spoke the words, she knew she was already giving herself the terrible news that Anne didn't want to deliver.

"She's not..."

"I'm sorry. Yes, your mum died about six months after your accident. I wasn't here back then but I've been told that she visited you every day she could, and she sat holding your hand the very day before she finally lost her battle with cancer."

This was Sophie's cue to cry. She knew she should be wailing with despair, but no tears came. All she could do was to watch Anne's tears trickle one by one down the side of her nose in that annoying tickly way and, as her chubby fingers dealt with each one in turn, she wished they were her own because that would mean that at least for now she would have behaved normally. The way any grieving daughter would if they weren't convinced this was nothing more than a bad dream.

She stared out of the window at the grey depressing sky and allowed herself for a moment to absorb the irony of it, bad dream or not. How she had done unthinkable things to protect her mum from facing her terminal illness, and instead, all she did was force her to go through it alone, alone and with the added heartbreak of seeing her only child in a self-inflicted coma.

She probably blamed herself. She probably spent the few months she had left in more agony than anyone could imagine.

There were no tears, not because anger and remorse had not yet given way to sadness but because she had spoken to her mum only a couple of days ago about Rebecca's sleep disorder, and that recent memory was far more powerful than some woman claiming she'd been dead for years.

Anne watched Sophie's reaction disapprovingly.

"What about dad?" It seemed important to distract her from her indignation.

Anne smiled and nodded "Yes your dad can't wait to come."

"And Kelly?" She expected that Anne would not have heard this name before.

"Yes, she is a regular visitor too."

"Really?"

"Yes really."

Instinctively she didn't ask for Niki. It was hard to dispel the feeling of disharmony between them even though the animosity had been caused by Carl's suicide and Carl was very much alive. Still, the feeling of guilt and the fear of retribution remained, causing her to stick with Kelly as a more amicable visitor.

It was pointless trying to convince these people that she really lived in another place, another world, because there was nothing whatsoever to gain. Either they were part of a non- existent world themselves, or they were her new reality and either way it would be stupid to cause them to question her sanity.

She asked for a mirror and reluctantly a nurse finally brought her a small hand mirror. She held it up confidently in protest to all the resistance, and defiantly held her composure when a stranger stared back at her from the glass.

She could barely recognise herself in the pale gaunt image but in some ways, she looked much younger than the mother of

Tori and Rebecca. Her skin was sickly white and drawn but the crow's feet had disappeared from the corners of her eyes along with the tiny hairline cracks from her upper lip.

Her hair was no more than a matted clump of furlike strands, lank, greasy and dull ending in the nape of her neck where it had obviously been hacked off periodically with household scissors.

She dropped the mirror onto the bed and put her hands up to feel her face and then along the length of her arms. The bones of her elbows protruded through the skin as though they might pop through with the slightest pressure, and the muscle of her upper arms she had worked so hard for at the gym, had gone leaving nothing but skin holding bones and veins together.

It was getting harder and harder to dismiss the fact that this was the body of a woman who had not moved out of this bed for some considerable time.

A nurse helped her into a wheelchair but sitting upright made her feel violently sick. It was like sea sickness of the worst kind.

"Perhaps you need to get back into bed and shower tomorrow?" The young nurse suggested, as she manoeuvred the chair back towards the bed.

"No!" Sophie protested, "I want to shower. I feel like a sewer. Can we just move more slowly?"

The chair crawled along the corridor inch by inch as Sophie clung to the chair arms to steady herself as though she were riding the waves of a stormy sea.

She was lifted gently onto a chair in the shower and as the warm water flowed over her, she sighed with the pleasure of it. She rested for a few moments between each movement as her hair was washed and conditioned, her body dried, and a clean gown wrapped around her skin covered skeleton.

After over an hour she was finally back in her bed, propped by pillows where she managed a few sips of the tea the nurse put to her lips.

Later that day her drip was removed, and the sickness started to subside a little as she finished a small bowl of soup. It was going to be a long uphill battle to get well again if she had to accept being trapped here for a while, but it wasn't a battle she was going to put any effort into. She would simply play along while she waited for the one special sleep that would undoubtedly return her to her rightful family. In the meantime, she was starting to feel almost a little entertained by the events unfolding before her.

Anne was constantly available, and she was beginning to wonder if the poor woman had any time off at all, but she seemed happy enough to be there and was obviously intrigued by Sophie's story. She insisted on being present when Sophie was reunited with her father and Kelly who were to visit later, and it crossed her mind that Anne was probably the envy of everyone in her profession at having landed a case like this.

She lay and watched the door as visitors arrived and started to spill along the corridor. They chatted as they passed her door while she searched the sea of faces hoping to recognise him. She heard the turn of the handle and the face of a grey-haired man peered through the glass. There was no mistaking him.

He looked greyer, older and much smaller than the man she had visited only a few days ago when she had taken the children to her parents' house. He was frail in comparison to the strong, jovial grandad who had thrown Tori into the air and caught her.

As she reached out and tried to hug away a decade of pain and missed memories from this pitiful version of her father, she couldn't decide if this was further proof that the other version was pure fantasy or, if grief, despair and heartbreak could be the cause of such physical devastation.

As he held her gently in his arms, she looked over his shoulder and caught sight of the tear filled big blue eyes still framed by false lashes, as they had been so many years ago. Kelly. The friend who had turned out to be the most loyal in both her worlds. She wondered if the relationship with the man she described as 'lovely' had stood the test of time, but she didn't mention it, as she couldn't quite remember where that conversation had taken place. Her worlds were starting to merge into one.

Sophie was the first to speak.

"So how is life for you two?" It was an open invitation for them to update her on anything at all.

Neither replied.

She looked to Kelly directly, and made the question more specific.

"Are you settled with anyone? Still avoiding love?"

Kelly was biting her lip extremely hard and seemed unable to say anything at all. This was clearly a shock for them, but she felt irritated that she was coping with much, much worse than either of them.

Kelly gave her a hug and eventually said "Oh. You know me. Heart of steel."

Sophie smiled at the irony of a woman speaking of her steel heart while tears of emotion poured through her muddy mascara

"Yes, I can see that."

Her father pushed Kelly aside a little while he had another hug and brushed her hair affectionately from her face.

"I love you so much and I never gave up on you."

"I know." Sophie was warming to him in his new form. He seemed more tender and compassionate than the version she had just left.

As Sophie looked her old friend up and down, noting her skinny jeans and vest top that showed off her gorgeous figure, she concluded that if a decade had really passed then fashion had not changed at all! Kelly took a tissue from the bedside stand with her perfectly manicured and moisturised hand and attempted to stem the flow of tears by dabbing gently under her eyes without disrupting her foundation too much. As quickly as she blotted each one away it was immediately replaced as she sobbed softly into the bunch of tissues accumulating in her hands.

"Welcome back. You crazy, stupid lady." She finally choked through the sobs.

"Thank you." Sophie picked up Kelly's hands and kissed each of them in turn.

"Do you know what happened?"

Kelly nodded but frowned in the direction of the old man as though suggesting they shouldn't talk of it in front of him.

Sophie nodded and allowed the subject to be changed.

Anne hovered awkwardly in the background, eves-dropping the conversation, always ready to interject if she felt a comment or act might hinder Sophie's recovery, but there was no need. Sophie was taking everything in her stride with her heart firmly fixated on her return to her real family. Most of the information being blurted out by her visitors was nothing more than white noise to her. She didn't need to retain any of it because soon it would be just a memory of another bad dream.

After the visitors left, she ate a sandwich which took almost half an hour as her tongue and jaw ached from the effort it took, and her throat laboured to push each chewed mouthful down to her stomach. Eventually the ordeal was over, and she lay down to sleep. She lay on her back and put out her arm to her right to feel for the place John had occupied so very recently. Her hand flopped dejectedly over the edge of her single bed as the clatter of the dinner trolly and the chatter of the canteen staff faded away and her eyes slowly closed.

The next morning, she could vaguely see the light through her eyelids when she felt the weight of a person beside her. Her heart quickened. Gingerly she stretched out her arm expecting it to fall over the edge of the bed but instead it fell onto something. Something warm and moving but before she could turn over, a face framed in black hair leaned over her.

"You had me worried there. You've slept for over twelve hours!" Anne laughed as she leaned back again but remained seated on Sophie's bed.

She wanted to punch Anne in her fat face. To rip it off for fooling her into thinking it might be John. To kill her for even existing.

"Leave me alone!" She barked, causing the poor woman to jump to her feet and take a step back.

She noticed Anne's demeanour change from shock to contempt as she looked sternly at Sophie's clenched fists. If she wasn't careful, she was about to get herself sedated again.

"Sorry. You made me jump. Can I have some time on my own please?"

Anne's face relaxed as she moved back towards the bed.

"Yes, of course. I'll call back in an hour or so."

Sophie was beyond disappointed. She thought she had touched John and now she felt desperately homesick. For a split second she had been back with her family and it caused her to worry about what was happening back there. Was time passing at the same rate as here or had it stood still? She hoped the children hadn't woken up to find her missing or unconscious or worse. She needed to get back there, and she needed to do it soon but until she could work out how, she was trapped and had to play the game. She couldn't risk being incarcerated.

As she tried to swallow some toast, she saw a flash of an old photo of herself on the tv screen in the next ward. Of course, she would have made the national news by now and as she tore off another chunk of crust she wondered if Anne was getting her fifteen minutes of fame out of it and if her poor dad was being harassed by reporters for being the father of the 'coma girl.'

"Is there anything specific you would like to ask me?" Anne was pulling up a chair as though settling in for a long conversation.

"What do you mean?"

"Well, there's over nine years of questions in your head I'm sure but rather than bombard you with information I think it would be easier for you, if you asked the things most important to you."

Sophie resisted the temptation to ask where the hell her family was and how could she get back there. How to escape this pantomime, with its bony body, strange child and dead boyfriend walking around, but instead she tried to think of something less contentious.

"Someone must have found me. Who was it?"

Anne sifted through the notes in her folder. It seemed that every detail of her life had been recorded in chronological order.

"It was Kelly. She called in to check on you when your dad said you had marched out of the hospital in a bit of a state" Anne was reading at first, but this question she already knew the answer to.

"She saw your car at the front, banged on the door and looked through the windows then went to the shed where your mum used to hide a key years ago."

"So, it's Kelly I need to thank?" She said in a manner that must have sounded genuine to Anne but held nothing other than sarcasm in Sophie's head as she cursed Kelly for being the interfering busy body.

"Yes, she told me about it yesterday when I took on your case. She said she blamed herself over the fact that she forgot to take her phone with her and lost vital time in raising the alarm. She didn't think to check your pockets for your own phone. Instead, she ran up the road trying to flag down cars and then knocked on doors, but no-one answered so many of them, until finally she managed to phone an ambulance. No-one knew exactly how long this took, or what impact had on you" Anne was carefully watching Sophie's reaction to the story.

"I think your parents blamed her a little too, for not checking your pockets".

"Poor Kelly," Sophie shook her head gently, "this wasn't her fault"

Anne nodded and then shrugged in a 'that's life' kind of way.

"And I was pregnant when I did this?" It was a rhetorical question.

"Yes. It's difficult to know what to do when someone's pregnant and unconscious, but the only moral thing is to let nature and your family decide, and your fiancé and parents were adamant about not aborting it. Your son was born by caesarean section and your fiancé was there at the birth to greet him for both of you. It says here that he insisted they put Tommy in your arms first. It seems you were the first to give him a cuddle."

Again, the tears Anne was expecting to see in Sophie's eyes, as she looked up were not there. They should have been there, Sophie knew that, but they just weren't. The only thoughts were the anger at Carl's inexhaustible bloody devotion. Perfect Carl. The one who did everything right while she did everything wrong. The one who honoured their love while she trashed it and the one who nurtured their child while she killed it. Perfect sodding Carl. The kind of man every woman dreams of. Every woman except her.

"The poor little mite has come to the ward almost every week, always bringing you something he had made for you, years of pictures and home-made birthday cards. They are all in a box in your locker, look at them when you feel ready to."

Sophie nodded and smiled. She had no intention of sifting through a hoard of infantile drawings from the boy who had replaced her daughters. The boy who had been tormenting her darling Rebecca.

"I'm going to give you your family back," Anne reassured, "I'll work with you every day until you are ready to go back to your life, don't worry."

If only Anne knew the ridiculous, cruel and somehow hilarious irony of her promise. She seemed to expect Sophie's gratitude as she continued.

"You should probably try to see him soon, for his sake. He's waited his whole life for this. Waiting and hoping his mummy would come back. You know that don't you? This is your baby, your son."

Sophie nodded again trying to imagine how she was going to gush love and tears over this boy she felt no connection with. Her real children were also waiting for her, or frozen in time somewhere, and her heart ached for them.

Anne seemed to read her thoughts.

"If you still have some illusion that your coma life is going to reappear then that's the first thing we need to work on, we need to take it off the table."

Sophie felt guilty that her secret thoughts had been so obvious "It's so hard."

"Of course it is," Anne patted her hand again which was starting to feel patronising, "you've been dreaming your own dreams for years and years. It must feel very real."

"It's more than that."

"Then tell me about it. Tell me about your husband."

Sophie smiled fondly. "His name is John. He's wonderful."

Anne smiled "Of course he is. If I were to invent a husband, I'd make him wonderful too!"

Sophie shook her head "He is real and he's the best."

"I bet he never insulted you?"

"No!"

"Never stayed late at work without telling you?"

"No!"

"Never had an affair or even looked at other women. Always supported you and told you how beautiful you were. Always called you darling and never complained about anything?"

"Yes but..."

"Sophie, men aren't like that. That's how we would like them to be, but they are inattentive, inconsiderate, womanising idiots most of the time and for the rest of it, they are plain dumb. You invented him, your perfect man."

"No, I didn't!" She yelled as she tried to think of something to throw back at this woman who was falling out of her favour very quickly. She pictured John and then gave a smug smile.

"Ok. So, if I invented him why isn't he a tall handsome muscle toned man with a six pack?" she said smugly.

Anne smiled "You didn't make him good looking? Clever move"

"I didn't make him at all!"

Anne was obviously trying very hard not to laugh.

"You didn't make him a physical God because in all the best love stories it's not the handsome man or beautiful girl who ends up happy. Love is meant to conquer all and that's the kind of love we crave, love built on something deeper and stronger than physical attraction. I bet he always turned up exactly when you needed him to?"

Sophie remembered him appearing in the rain in her most desperate hour and was getting more and more annoyed.

"Stop it! Stop it! You're trying to make me give up on my husband and I won't let you."

"Ok. Have it your own way, but think about it a little. How could anyone be that perfect?"

"My children aren't perfect. Rebecca is disturbed, she has terrible dreams of another life just like I did. Back when the whole thing started."

Anne was trying to edge away and leave her alone with her thoughts but on hearing this interesting revelation she sat back down.

"That's interesting. You used to have dreams that felt real before this?"

"Yes," Sophie admitted, "I was having them before I took the overdose."

"Do you think the dreams may have had some bearing on what you did?"

Sophie laughed.

"It was the dreams that drove me to do it. I was also depressed and very confused, but I was desperate to escape the life I was stuck in....... this damn life!"

Anne was scribbling notes enthusiastically. Sophie's case had the potential to get her published in the medical journal.

"Are you still convinced there's another life waiting for you or have you accepted it wasn't ever real?"

"Oh, it's real alright, and now Rebecca has the same affliction, or do you think I made that up too?"

Anne was still scribbling.

"It's possible. It's likely that your fear of your own problem was constantly in your mind while you were in this semi-conscious state and so it was transferred to the new version of yourself, your daughter."

"I don't think I would have made her ill on purpose. She talks to someone called Tommy. Don't you see? it all makes some sort of weird sense."

Anne smiled "That's because you have heard Tommy's name repeatedly over the years. Whispering into your sub-conscious. I would have been amazed if he hadn't managed to infiltrate your dreams!"

"But if I was inventing my perfect life, why would I invent a disturbed daughter?"

"Not all dreams are good ones. You should know that. We sometimes have nightmares, but they all come from our own heads, all in our own control really."

"Well, the only nightmare is the one I'm in right now."

"So, tell me how the dream problem started. Right from the beginning."

Sophie started at the very beginning, right from the moment she told her friends of the kind of love she wanted in the lively bar one Friday night and as she talked and listened to herself, she could feel the whole story starting to make sense. Each element unravelling one after the other of the fantasy life she'd craved.

Until this conversation with Anne, she had been harbouring thoughts of suicide again as a way of returning, but she knew her plan was flawed. Her previous attempt had not resulted in death but in a coma. A coma that probably was a similar state of mind to the sleep that had effectively carried her back and forth from the start.

As her story unfolded and Anne patted her hand again, this time it was welcomed as there was only one conclusion she could make when she compared her lardlike translucent flesh to the plump pink hand above it. She had missed her own life, her real life, the years with Carl and her son. She tried to fight it, but little by little she could feel that she was allowing herself to start to let go of her beloved John, of Tori and Rebecca, of any life other than this one.

"Sedate me!" She said suddenly.

"What?"

"Sedate me. It might work. Sleep doesn't take me anywhere anymore, but the coma did. I feel like I need to go deeper or something. Perhaps if you sedate me?"

Anne shook her head, but she couldn't hide the excitement Sophie had stirred up.

"I'm not your medical doctor for a start and your doctor isn't going to randomly sedate you just to see if you dream the same dream."

"So, what will get me sedated?" Sophie asked as she tipped over a chair "This?"

"Or this?" she threw her dinner tray across the room and ran at the drugs trolley screaming as she tipped the whole thing over, scattering controlled drugs down the corridor like spilt smarties. She was pulling pillows from behind patients and throwing them into the air when two nurses overpowered her and called for help.

"Doctor!"

Sophie saw a white coat striding down the corridor under the straggles of her hair that had fallen over her face.

"Nurse, sedation please!"

"Don't give her much," Anne pleaded, "I'll be able to calm her, it was just momentary frustration."

The doctor administered only half of what had been drawn into the syringe and frowned at Anne.

"She'll be out for twenty minutes."

Anne nodded "I'll keep an eye on her."

They guided Sophie back onto the bed as she started to relax and close her eyes.

"I've never seen that before," the doctor added, "she actually stayed still while I injected her."

Anne smiled and muttered silently to herself, "Of course she did."

She picked up the overturned chair and pulled it beside Sophie's bed as she felt her wrist. Her heartbeat was slow and regular, so she made herself comfortable and watched Sophie sleep.

After a few minutes she could see her eyeballs moving under her lids. She moved closer to watch and checked her wrist again. Her heart was beating faster now, despite the sedation, and her eyelids were dancing frantically as though she was desperately searching left and right. Suddenly they stopped moving as though she was staring at something and she seemed to hold her breath.

Her heart was still racing as her lids started moving again but this time more slowly almost sadly, but her heart was still gaining pace as she started to pummel the rails of the bed with her fists. She considered calling for the doctor, but she didn't want to disturb whatever was happening to Sophie, because she knew it was something unique. Something no other psychologist had written about. She held her ground and watched the dancing eyelids, the pounding fists and the contorted face until eventually the eyelids started to open.

Sophie stared up at the ceiling without speaking.

"Sophie? Sophie are you alright?"

Slowly she turned her head in Anne's direction as though unsure of her surroundings and then started to cry.

Anne put her notepad on the mobile tray and sat beside Sophie on the bed.

"What happened?"

For a few moments she cried into her pillow and then stared up at Anne with a look of desperation in her eyes.

"I have to go back to them. I have to go now!"

"Did you see them?" Anne wished her notepad was a bit nearer.

"Yes, but they couldn't hear me. I shouted and shouted at John. He had Tori in his arms and Becky clung to him like she was scared to death, but they couldn't hear me. It was like they were behind glass."

Anne couldn't help herself, she had to write it down.

"Just a minute, let me get my pad. All this may be useful to you."

As Anne scribbled again, Sophie continued.

"At one-point John looked right at me and said something, but I couldn't hear him either. He seemed to be beside water, a lake or something. I thought he was going to walk into the lake with my kids, so I banged on the glass. I banged and banged."

She looked down at her swollen, red fists.

"Look! Look Anne! My fists! It was real. You can't deny it now. Look. You can see the proof."

She took Sophie's swollen hand in hers and sighed deeply.

"I'm sorry love. You bruised your hands on the bed rails. I sat here and watched you punching them."

Anne's words took the wind from her sails. She wasn't sure of anything. She once again had to consider the possibility that she'd experienced a bad dream and nothing more. That this life might be her only life. Perhaps she had to make the best of it. At least in this life she wasn't guilty of aborting her child or of causing Carl's suicide and her friends didn't hate her.

She thought of Kelly. Faithful devoted Kelly who'd hardly left her side and had helped to care for her child while she waited patiently for her to wake up. Kelly had been an angel. Foolishly she allowed her heart to fill with gratitude and love for Kelly. The reality was that she couldn't have been further from the truth.

She lay back down on the bed, closed her eyes for a moment and imagined John's face again. It felt real. As real as the life she had lived with him. Her children had looked terrified as they clung to their dad. She could feel her back becoming moist with sweat as the instinct of a mother to protect her children rose to the surface again.

She was not going to accept that there were no children awaiting her return, no perfect husband with a broken heart or no wonderful mum still alive and well. They all needed her, and they needed her now.

"I want to be alone for a bit."

Anne left her without protest.

From the side of her bed, Sophie picked up a pen and notepad. She was going to get back to John and her girls. She had done it before, and she would do it again. All she needed to do was to work out how to get there and how to stay there and recording every damn thing she could remember was the most likely way for her to find a common denominator.

The secret to getting back into his arms for real and for good, not behind some glass barrier and not to be pulled back here again. She tore off a page and started to meticulously write down every detail from the moment she woke up on that first Monday to make her presentation.

The answer was somewhere in the exact circumstances or sequence of events, she was sure of it.

She tore off another page and continued. Writing and tearing, writing and tearing and as she did so she made a vow never to stop until she could feel John's arms around her again. She made her vow with no concept of the pain and horror it would eventually deliver or the terrors that lay ahead.

It didn't matter. The only thing that mattered was John's love and her daughters.

Anne returned quietly and stood at the door un-noticed. Her heart fluttered as she watched the wide-eyed woman frantically scribbling on the bits of paper that were now littering her bed.

This was a familiar sight to her. She had seen this kind of madness before and it hadn't ended well. She had hoped to save Sophie from similar incarceration. From a similar demise. From the same tragic ending.

Sophie spotted her in the doorway, standing there, with her pitying expression. She looked the plump little woman directly in the face and smiled widely. It was of no consequence what Anne thought.

She was going home.

Printed in Great Britain
by Amazon